"We've got three weeks to make arrangements before our wedding day."

"Rozzano!" Sophia cried in horror. "We can't get married that soon! It's crazy. Six months would be much more sensible—"

"Sensible! Who wants to be sensible?" His eyes glittered.

"Marriage is for keeps, Rozzano. It would be awful if we made a mistake."

"*Four* weeks, then!" he said forcefully. "You can't possibly ask me to wait any longer! We want to be together, don't we?" He turned her face and lovingly, lingeringly, kissed her mouth. "We'll be perfect together, Sophia. I know we will. So," he said, smiling fondly at her, "we'd better start planning the wedding of the decade!"

Harlequin Presents® invites you to see how the other half marries in:

SOCIETY WEDDINGS

*They're gorgeous, they're glamorous...
and they're getting married!*

In this sensational five-book miniseries you'll be our VIP guest at some of the most talked-about weddings of the decade— spectacular events where the cream of society gather to celebrate the marriages of dazzling brides and grooms in equally breathtaking, international locations.

At each of these lavish ceremonies you'll meet some extra-special men and women—all rich, royal or just renowned!—whose stories are guaranteed to capture your imagination, your hearts...and the headlines! For in this sophisticated world of fame and fortune you can be sure of one thing: there'll be no end of scandal, surprises...and passion!

We know you'll enjoy Sara Wood's
The Impatient Groom.

Next month, join us in a toast to another happy couple in:
The Mistress Bride (#2056)
by
Michelle Reid

SARA WOOD

The Impatient Groom

SOCIETY WEDDINGS

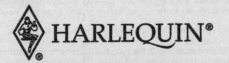

HARLEQUIN®

TORONTO • NEW YORK • LONDON
AMSTERDAM • PARIS • SYDNEY • HAMBURG
STOCKHOLM • ATHENS • TOKYO • MILAN • MADRID
PRAGUE • WARSAW • BUDAPEST • AUCKLAND

ISBN 0-373-12054-0

THE IMPATIENT GROOM

First North American Publication 1999.

Visit us at www.romance.net

Printed in U.S.A.

CHAPTER ONE

FROM the shadows of the musicians' gallery, Rozzano watched his sister-in-law's birthday celebrations and fought a losing battle against the inevitable. He just *had* to marry. It was an appalling idea—but he couldn't face the alternative. A vicious claw of pain dragged at his stomach.

In the beautiful eighteenth-century ballroom below, high-maintenance mistresses were performing prettily for their well-heeled lovers and dazzling beauties purred in the arms of elderly tycoons. Several guests were roaming around and slyly fingering the antiques in an attempt to price them.

His chest inflated with a tight, angry breath. These were *his* possessions, his palace—and these people were defiling them. He despised the crowd his brother ran around with. Tawdry, the lot of them.

And in the midst of the excited, empty chatter his lying, cheating, work-shy brother swaggered like a peacock, flaunting himself and the wealth of the Barsinis while the birthday girl bitched in a corner and her spoilt children screamed and squabbled and stuffed themselves with expensive delicacies.

Prince Rozzano Alessandro di Barsini allowed himself the rare luxury of a malevolent scowl. He had a reputation for being the perfect, urbane gentleman. It would astonish people if they could ever see him otherwise. But Barsini emotions were not for public display.

'Have emotions if you must!' his father had said on

one memorable occasion. 'But have the decency to keep them to yourself!'

So all the consuming hatred and fury he felt for his relations had been kept totally private—but, hell, was it good to let the mask slip for a few moments!

Tonight, being polite to everyone for the last hour had tested his patience to breaking point and he was finding it harder and harder to restrain himself in the face of his brother's excesses. As a child, he had spent painful long hours in isolation, forcing his volcanic passions into the required strait-jacket shaped by his exacting father. After thirty-four years of self-discipline, he had learned his lesson well.

He'd coped by diverting his explosive energies to high-danger, high-energy sports that demanded that he push himself to the limit. But increasingly there were times when Enrico went too far and Rozzano's control was sorely tried.

Contempt tore at his sensual mouth. He found his brother repulsive, vulgar and immoral. Even now, Enrico was caressing a woman's back. She was married, with two children—one of the many mistresses Enrico supported. An impotent fury surged through him like a burning acid that his brother should flaunt the woman in the family *palazzo*!

He thought of the day Enrico had been born and how the tiny, black-haired scrap of humanity had melted his heart. Enrico had seemed like a miracle to him. But he'd been four years old then, and unaware that the innocent gurgling baby would systematically poison the lives of everyone he came in contact with—just for the sheer hell of it.

Rozzano went pale. The poison was in him too. It grieved him to feel such extreme anger and revulsion for someone of his own blood—but he could never forgive Enrico for what he'd done. Not ever.

He set his jaw in determination, knowing he had no choice but to take drastic action. Otherwise he didn't know what the devil he was going to do about Enrico—how to curb him, help him, and ensure he did no more damage to the unwary.

Only yesterday he'd tried to talk some sense into him. Enrico had laughed and said that life was for living and who but a fool wanted to work in an office all day? He fumed at the memory. Did his brother imagine that a publishing empire ran itself?

Turning away in rage when some drunken guests collided and knocked over a valuable medieval candle-stand, Rozzano hardened his heart.

As the elder son of one of the most ancient and noble Venetian families, he had a duty to protect the honour—and the survival—of the Barsini name. Enrico and his loathsome brats must not take the title in the event of his death.

He needed an heir. There was no escape then. He had to find a wife. Rozzano drew in a harsh breath, shaken by the finality of the decision he'd made.

Slowly his fingers curled, shaping his finely shaped hands into belligerent fists. He swallowed back the bile that had risen to his throat and groaned. What he did for this family!

Turbulent emotions battled for his heart and mind. He'd vowed not to become involved with a woman ever again. Four years, three months and four days ago, to be precise. He knew that moment of his wife's death almost to the hour! His even white teeth savaged his lower lip as he struggled for self-control.

A searing black venom blazed in his eyes as bitter

resentment fuelled his loathing. Because of the part
Enrico had played in his wife's death, he would have to
throw himself on the marriage market again. He'd be
forced to choose a woman he didn't love—couldn't
love—and he'd have to play the doting husband for the
rest of his life. What a sentence!

Grim-faced, he thought of the women he knew, the
ones who adored him, the many who flirted and were
more than willing. He'd give none of them house room.

'Damn you, Enrico!' he ground out through his teeth.
Happiness would continue to evade him. He had everything—and he had nothing. Except the fatherly affection
of an old man.

He groaned. D'Antiga! He'd almost forgotten!

The church clock chimed and he checked his Cartier
watch with a sharp exclamation. First things first. He
must leave.

Somewhere in southern England, a solicitor waited
with news of D'Antiga's fortunes—and this alone had
intrigued him enough to draw him half-way across
Europe. Maybe they'd found D'Antiga's runaway daughter! If so, he would not be obliged to run the D'Antiga
estates any longer, on behalf of his late father's friend.

His expression became smooth and implacable again.
His passionate anger was ruthlessly suppressed. Thought-
fully, Rozzano began to descend the gilded stairway.
Maybe he could take back the reins of the Barsini publishing house from his brother and get it running
smoothly again!

Exhilarated at the prospect, he headed for the watergate. A nod of his head brought the waiting servants to
life, one hurrying to alert his boatman, one passing him
his long wool coat, briefcase and gloves.

As always, others smoothed his path for the whole of

the tedious journey. When he left his *palazzo* he travelled by motor launch to Venice's airport for the flight to London. After a night in his suite at the Dorchester, a chauffeured car took him to the private plane, which conveyed him to an airport on the south coast of England. From there he was driven to a small village in Dorset called Barley Magma.

Il Principe Rozzano Alessandro di Barsini stepped from his hire car looking as immaculate and composed as if he'd just woken and dressed ten minutes earlier.

But even before breakfast he'd dealt with yet another crisis of Enrico's making, spoken at length to his broker and taken several calls from his publishing outlets around the world. In the car he'd dealt with urgent papers, switching his mind with alacrity from his own affairs to those of D'Antiga's perfumeries.

'Yup, that's it,' encouraged the hire driver when he hesitated.

They'd stopped outside a tiny grocer's shop on the end of a terrace of houses whose golden stone was glowing softly in the September sunshine. A perplexed frown fleetingly dared to spoil the smoothness of Rozzano's high, broad forehead and irritation tightened his jaw. A fool's errand, then. A mistake. He felt the disappointment keenly.

Abruptly he turned back to the car. 'I have no business with a grocer.'

'Nah! The solicitor rents rooms above,' the driver told him cheerfully. He knew wealth when he saw it and anticipated a fat tip. 'Door round the corner.'

Still doubtful, Rozzano nevertheless thanked him politely. This didn't look hopeful. 'Come back for me, if you please. Say…an hour?'

He thought he'd be out before that, but he could always sit beneath the large oak tree and work on his papers. Quickly he strode to the open door at the side of the building. His face showed no hint of his thoughts, which were that there was surely a mix-up.

How, he wondered, as his hand-stitched leather shoes trod each uncarpeted step upwards, could a small-time solicitor in a rural backwater have any connection with the Venetian aristocracy? Let alone solve a thirty-three-year-old mystery!

His hopes fading, he entered the poorly appointed office. A young woman at a desk seemed to be trying to type and gossip on the telephone simultaneously. Without looking up she covered the mouthpiece and snapped a scratchy, 'Yes?'

His dark eyes narrowed but his tone remained civil and very—perhaps ominously—quiet as he approached her desk.

'Good morning. I have an appointment. Rozzano Barsini—'

'Oh! The prince!' The woman dropped the phone in shock, blushed scarlet and knocked over a pile of files and a mug of coffee, causing Rozzano to step back quickly before his sharply tailored jacket was ruined. 'Blast! Oh, I'm sorry, Your—um—Highness!' In confusion, she tried to mop up the mess, apologise and stare in awe all at the same time.

He handed over his soft linen handkerchief, hoping wryly that she wouldn't curtsey. Her knees looked alarmingly poised to do so.

'Please calm yourself,' he said, wearied with the effect his name invariably produced.

He was an unwilling celebrity. Since his wife's death, the media had been obsessed with his life, reporting every minor detail—and the partying extravagances of his brother. Rozzano controlled the urge to say bitingly that column inches in a newspaper didn't make someone a god.

'I'll wait till you're ready to announce me,' he said instead, his voice stiff with restraint.

The secretary cleared up, then flapped and fluttered her way to an inner office from where he could hear an excited conversation developing.

Suppressing a sigh, Rozzano cast a doubtful eye over a rather tired-looking sofa and, easing the knife creases of his dark navy trousers, made himself as comfortable as possible on a rickety wooden chair. Wishing he hadn't wasted his valuable time, he reached for his phone, to make a few calls.

Only then did he notice the woman sitting by the window. 'Excuse me! I thought I was alone. Good morning,' he said politely, tucking his mobile phone back in its slimline holster at his waist.

She acknowledged him with a smile that softened her sooty grey eyes. 'Morning,' she replied easily.

Her voice was so low and lyrical and warmly welcoming that it immediately had the effect of soothing his irritation.

She must have been aware of who he was, because the secretary had screeched it to the Four Winds, but she seemed relaxed and apparently unimpressed. It was a pleasant change. He looked away out of habit, because up to now he'd avoided possible entanglements with women like the plague, but her reaction had been so surprising that he gave her a second glance.

An amused smile lifted the corners of his mouth and softened his stern features. He'd been forgotten—or dismissed! It was such a novelty that he found himself both intrigued and enchanted.

She was looking out onto the street, her blissful expression suggesting she was dreaming of something delightful. With some regret, Rozzano remembered his manners and turned away again, but not before he'd been deeply struck by the gentle repose of her face and body.

Unlike the fashionably tiny and bean-thin young women he knew, she was quite tall, large-boned and curvaceous—a kind of homely earth-mother type. And yet…

Pretending to flick through an ancient bridal magazine, he tried to work out what was puzzling him. Her clothes, maybe? He'd retained an impression of an ill-fitting gentian-blue polyester dress that sagged at the hem, and a caramel brown cardigan of an uncertain age and style. He hadn't missed those incredible legs, though—long, slender and bare, tanned to a gleaming, smooth gold and with ankles so shapely that he could pleasurably imagine his hands curving around them. Yet she wore old-fashioned and poorly made shoes—although, he conceded, they'd been well polished. And her rich toffee-coloured hair had been dragged back from her face into a tight, thick plait as if she disapproved of frivolity.

Nothing there, then, other than those legs, to make the heart beat faster. In that case, what had caught his attention, what was so utterly fascinating? Riveted, he put his mind to the conundrum.

Allora. He had it! Excitement glittered in the depths of his shadowed dark eyes. Incongruously, an air of refinement pervaded her whole body. It revealed itself in her perfect posture—the ramrod-straight back, the graceful carriage of her head with its delicate, almost fragile features, and the demure arrangement of those staggeringly beautiful legs.

Interesting. Perhaps he'd strike up a conversation, he thought with idle curiosity...

'Mr Luscombe's ready for you now, Your Highness!' the secretary announced loudly, too loudly, her eyes shining with excitement.

'Thank you.'

Astonished that he felt annoyed because he hadn't been able to speak to the blissfully unaware Madonna, Rozzano brought his interest under control, rose and strolled at his usual leisurely pace into Luscombe's office. As the elderly solicitor greeted him, he heard the secretary add sneeringly, dismissively, 'Oh, and you're to come in too, Miss Charlton.'

He swivelled on his heel, startled. The serene, dreaming Madonna had indeed followed him in! What the hell had she to do with the D'Antiga millions?

'Would you like coffee, Your Highness?' suggested the secretary, in a sickeningly unctuous voice.

He shot her a hard look. 'In my country,' he said softly, pained that he felt driven to make the rebuke, 'women take priority over men.'

'Yes, Jean, bring coffee for everyone!' The solicitor's glare at his secretary said it all.

And then Luscombe turned his attention to the seraphic woman behind Rozzano. As the solicitor drew her forward and welcomed her, the anger in his face melted away and he was all smiles.

So was Rozzano, though he wasn't sure why. Smiling hadn't been in his repertoire of expressions for a long time, but when he looked at the Madonna it just happened. While she solemnly shook the solicitor's hand, he reflected that her very presence seemed to have a balmy effect on his seething brain.

As Frank Luscombe completed the introductions,

Rozzano took Sophia Charlton's slender and graceful hand and, on a totally uncharacteristic and flamboyant impulse, bent low to kiss it.

He looked and smelled gorgeous, she thought, staring at the top of his smooth, dark head and still trying to recall where she'd heard his name before. Since he was a prince, she supposed that she must have read about him attending some jet-set party or a film premiere. How glamorous!

And then his eyes lifted to hers—warm, inky-black and magnetic. Sophia was startled. This was no playboy. He had depth. Intelligence.

A glow relaxed all her muscles, the same inner glow she'd felt when he'd first walked into the waiting room and she'd heard his rich, chocolate-syrup voice and its intriguing accent.

His arrival had prompted her to dream of meeting *her* prince one day, falling in love and having his children. Even if that 'prince' turned out to be a farmhand or an estate agent, he'd be a prince to *her*!

And they'd have children. Four would be perfect. Sophia sighed. She longed for a baby. The desire had grown more urgent as her biological clock had begun to tick away. Although she'd always made the best of whatever situation she was in, a family would make her life complete.

Humour and common sense dragged her back to reality. Out here in this quiet country setting, white horses bearing spare bachelor princes, farmhands or estate agents were thin on the ground. Especially ones who'd fall madly in love with a thirty-two-year-old spinster in a terminally ill brown cardy!

Amused, she imagined Prince Rozzano leaning down

from his white stallion and hooking her up to sit in front of him. He'd unbutton her demure cardigan and fling it away in a fit of unbridled passion.

She stifled a giggle and paid attention, her face as sombre as she could make it.

'So please, take a seat. And I must apologise for Jean,' Frank was saying. 'She's a temp. My own secretary is on maternity leave.'

'How lovely!' she said, suppressing her envy. 'But I'm sure it's been difficult for you,' Sophia sympathised.

She sat down and tried to make her too short skirt cover a bit more thigh. The prince had already given her legs a couple of glances. Unfortunately she couldn't tell if he'd disapproved or enjoyed the experience.

The secretary knocked on the door and placed a tray on the solicitor's desk, her hands clumsily knocking against the phone as she did so. Simpering, she handed the prince a cup, looked disappointed when he coolly declined her further services via milk and sugar and stalked out in a sulk, leaving Sophia and Frank to reach for their own less than pristine mugs.

Frank sighed. 'I give up!'

Sophia's eyes were laughing at his mock despair. 'If you're stuck any time in the future, I could always pop in and give you a hand,' she offered. 'I used to do Father's typing and accounts for him.'

Frank looked bemused. 'I thought you ran a day nursery before you stopped working to care for him?'

Her face grew soft with the happy memories of those days. 'I did. I adored it, too,' she admitted. 'But I helped Father in my spare time. Frankly, I'd do anything now— so long as it doesn't involve night or daylight robbery, pushing drugs or—' She stopped, realising she'd gabbled on without her usual sense of caution. This definitely wasn't the place to mention prostitution!

'Or?' prompted the prince.

'Anything illegal.' She made the words as prim as possible.

'Ah.'

From the look in his eyes, it was plain that he knew exactly what she'd meant! Demurely she continued. 'Apart from the voluntary work I do at the school, I've been out of work since Father died.' She grimaced. 'You know what it's like finding a job here, Frank. If I lived in a town it would be easier, but I can't afford to move.'

A low laugh escaped when she remembered her last attempt at finding employment.

'Share it, please, Miss Charlton,' murmured the prince, the expression in his eyes veiled by his impossibly long lashes.

Both men seemed interested, so she gave a shrug and shared. 'I was desperate for any kind of work,' she told them solemnly, 'so last week I applied for a job as a bin man—*person*,' she corrected, remembering to be politically correct.

'Bin…person?'

The prince's English was amazing, but obviously aristocrats didn't know about such things. Solemnly she explained. 'Refuse collector.'

The prince's only response was a millimetre lift of his eyebrows. Not a man to wear his humour on his sleeve, then. She was seized by a wicked desire to shock him, or to force a smile to crack that composure.

Frank was more forthcoming. 'And?' he queried, grinning.

'Looking around at the competition, I thought I had a good chance,' she said, keeping her expression deadpan.

'Then in came a guy with a shaven head, tattoos and a vest, bursting at the seams with Herculean muscles. I knew all was lost. Given an hour or two I could manage the first three of those, but not the last!'

Frank laughed. She thought the prince was smiling, but she kept her eyes firmly ahead. For some reason he was making her feel edgy. What could he possibly have to do with her?

'I think,' Frank observed, still chuckling, 'you'll soon have better things to do than to collect other people's rubbish.'

The prince leaned forward a fraction. Sophia treated herself to a quick glance. From the slight lift of his shoulders she deduced that he was tense, even though no such emotion showed on the perfection of his smooth, olive-skinned face.

But as a vicar's daughter she'd had practice in reading small gestures. Perception came with the job. How else did you know when a widower was being brave but really wanted to talk and weep over his bereavement? Or that the jar of home-made jam, which one of the parishioners had brought in, was only an excuse for needing a heart-to-heart about their wayward daughter?

Her wandering mind suddenly snapped back, to focus on the present situation. And suddenly she was tense too, wondering how an Italian nobleman fitted in with Frank's mysterious phone call, which had promised she would hear something to her advantage.

'Like…the offer of a job as a nursery nurse?' she had asked hopefully.

'Much better,' was all Frank would say at the time.

But that was what she wanted—to return to the career she'd adored, surrounded by children, loving them, mothering them.

'Sophia?'

Her hand went to her mouth in dismay and then she gave a small laugh of apology, used to missing conversations when she retreated into her inner fantasy world.

'Sorry! I'm a terrible drifter!' she said amiably.

'Thinking of Hercules and his vest?' suggested the prince.

Her eyes twinkled. Beneath that cool exterior lurked a decent sense of humour! She felt irrationally pleased.

'I was thinking of children,' she told him, with unconscious tenderness. 'I wish I could find work with them.'

Frank coughed meaningfully but his eyes were smiling at her in a kindly way. Reluctantly she pushed back the memories of the blissful times she'd spent with the kiddies in her care.

'Yes, I'm listening!' She sat very calmly, her hands in her lap. 'Go ahead.'

The solicitor fussily squared the sheaf of papers in front of him. 'Let me see…Where to start?'

She sensed that the prince had become unnaturally still. Her glance flicked across to him again. He had a strong and hard profile, which suggested a ruthless determination.

In her judgement, he was ruthless with himself, too. The line of his hair at the nape of his neck was unnaturally neat, his collar too dazzling, the set of his tie so exact that it might have been glued in place after careful positioning with the aid of a set square and ruler.

Then she spotted that a small, wayward curl was flicking around his ear in defiance of his attempted perfection. She felt a wicked pleasure at its mutiny. This man was so immaculately turned out, he might have been carved in marble—clothes and all!

He looked at her then. To her delight his mouth wid-

ened into a broad smile in response to hers. She was
totally disarmed, as if he was awarding her a rare privi-
lege.

She felt an almost irrepressible urge to tousle his hair.
It would look marvellous streaming back from his face
in the wind. She could see him now, on nearby Barley
Hill, the sun highlighting that incredible bone structure.

'Are you as impatient as I to know what strange quirk
of fate should bring us together in this office?' he asked
her.

His mellow, cultured voice slid deliciously through
her. She wallowed in the sensation while pretending to
be considering his remark. It was a rarity having a prince
turn her insides to treacle and she meant to enjoy every
melting second.

'Not impatient. I'm sure Frank will tell us in his own
good time,' she said good-naturedly. Anyone who'd sat
through vicarage teas with long-winded parishioners
knew the meaning of patience. 'But it does seem extraordinary!'

'My thoughts entirely.'

More than extraordinary, she decided. Improbable!
They were from different planets. His clothes certainly
were. They fitted his superb body so well that they must
have been made for him. The neat line of his broad shoulders was a work of art in itself. More set squares and
rulers, she supposed.

His carefully groomed hair and manicured nails suggested a man who had time to spend on himself—or he
paid others to take care of his appearance for him. All
that and a title too. Other than chalk and cheese, how
different could you get?

Sophia leant towards him and whispered on impulse,
'I think Frank's got his files mixed up, to be honest.'

He smiled, his eyes softening in a way that made the breath catch in her throat. 'That had crossed my mind.'

'Won't be long,' Frank muttered, preoccupied with his papers. 'Just looking for something…'

He looked excited. Sophia frowned. When ever did solicitors lose their cool? Frank's tension communicated itself to her and a sudden attack of nerves made her fill the painful silence and blurt out to the prince, 'Do you think I might be your long-lost sister?'

His eyes flickered over her from head to toe and a heat followed his leisurely appraisal, coursing down her body as if a blazing torch had blasted it.

'I think that's unlikely, don't you?' he murmured, staring at her ankles as if they alone proved she had no aristocratic bones in her body.

'It was a joke,' she mumbled, disconcerted by what was happening to her.

The dark chocolate eyes lifted to hers languidly. 'I know.'

He stared harder, frowning, examining in detail her face and mouth. Then he drew in a harsh breath and jerked himself to the edge of his seat as if something amazing had suddenly occurred to him.

'Mr Luscombe!' he shot out abruptly, all princely charm vanishing with a startling suddenness. 'You told me on the telephone that you had news concerning my father's friend D'Antiga. Are we talking about his daughter?'

'In a way,' said Frank, flustered. 'But—'

'She's dead, I presume.'

Frank frowned, obviously taken aback by the prince's suddenly curt manner. 'You've guessed right, but if I may—'

'Was there a child?'

Frank shifted uncomfortably and looked as if he'd been put on the spot. 'Please, let me break this as gently as I can—'

'Break what?' Sophia cried in sudden alarm. 'Why do you have to be gentle? And what's the connection between Prince Rozzano and me?' she insisted, beginning to panic.

As she spoke, she remembered where she'd heard his name before. Some time ago, there had been a picture of him on the front page of every tabloid in the newsagent's. It had been an image of utter grief. His harrowed face had roused pity in her, she recalled.

The memory of that photo haunted her but the reason remained elusive. What had it been? And did it have any bearing on why he was here?

'Sophia, my dear.'

'Yes? Oh. Sorry.' Her wavering attention was caught by the solicitor's kindly tones. That increased her anxiety. He was about to tell her something unnerving. 'What is it? What's wrong?' she asked, her face pale with apprehension.

'It's now eleven months since your father died.'

'Yes, Frank, I know—'

'For the prince's benefit, I need to say this.' Frank turned to the prince to explain further. 'He suffered from multiple sclerosis. Sophia was his full-time carer for the last six years.'

The prince looked grave, his eyes remaining on hers for several seconds as if he found the information interesting. 'That's a long time.'

She looked from Frank to Rozzano, afraid of the reason for their concern. 'Please get on with it!' she begged, her lips dry and stiff.

Frank sat back in his chair with a smug expression.

'Probate of your father's will is now complete, Sophia,' he said, excitement threading through every word. 'It was unusually complicated.' Frank cleared his throat. 'Sophia…he kept a secret. Your mother's secret. She made him promise never to reveal it to you. Being a man of integrity, he kept his word. But just before his death he asked me to put you in the picture when I judged that you were ready. He thought you should know the secret because he loved you and wanted you to be given the chance to—'

The prince made her jump by exclaiming sharply in Italian. As if unable to contain himself, he sprang to his feet and began to pace up and down, his beautifully cut jacket flaring open to reveal a pale gold silk waistcoat hugging his lithe figure.

Totally unnerved by Rozzano's reaction, Sophia turned back to Frank in desperation.

'The chance to what?' she asked plaintively, dismayed at the small, betraying shake in every word.

Rozzano spun around, an undercurrent of excitement spilling into his voice and sparking his dark eyes so that they flashed brilliantly. 'Can't you see she's desperate to know, beneath that very English restraint?' he said in fast, harsh tones. 'I know who she is. She's Violetta's daughter, isn't she? Violetta D'Antiga!'

'Spot on!' cried Frank, as pleased as punch.

Sophia's apprehension evaporated in a flash. They were both way off the mark! She relaxed back in her seat in relief.

'Well! You got my nerves hopping for nothing! Mother's name was Violet Charlton!' She realised that Frank must be so overworked, he was losing his grip! 'You definitely need a good secretary, Frank, to sort your files,' she chided. 'I knew there was a mix-up!'

And then, to her amazement, the prince was kneeling at her feet, his hands taking hers. Their eyes met, hers huge and uncomprehending, his fierce and bright.

She found herself trembling at his nearness. But that wasn't surprising. He was a dish. An immensely compelling man. Any woman alive would have wilted after glimpsing the raw, driving energy that he kept locked up behind that urbane exterior.

It was scary. And she found it shockingly exciting in a disturbing, sexual way. That, she thought wryly, was the trouble with living a cloistered, sheltered existence. You didn't often come across men oozing effortless sexual desire in villages boasting one post office and a duck pond.

'There's no mistake. We are linked,' he said simply.

Linked. For a brief moment, Sophia's breath seemed to have left her body. Electricity seemed to be surging between them as if there was, indeed, a vital connection. And then she grinned shakily because it was so unbelievable—both the connection and the two-way electricity!

What a fool she was! Vicar's daughter meets Sex On Legs. She was bound to be overwhelmed! She chuckled.

'Of course,' she agreed. 'An Italian prince in head-to-toe Armani—'

'Gianfranco Ferre,' he corrected her in surprise, as if any fool could have identified the style of his elegant suit.

'OK, Ferre—how am I to know?' she said mildly. 'Anyway, you're telling me that a prince, and an impoverished vicar's daughter in hand-me-downs are *linked*?' she finished in mock astonishment, her eyes alive with inner laughter.

'A vicar,' he mused, his black-lashed gaze taking in every feature of her face. 'That explains a good deal.'

'Well, explain it to me!' she suggested, quickly concealing a small tremor of her lower lip.

Her face was tingling where his breath had whispered across it. It felt as if he'd caressed it with his hand...or his mouth. Her eyes became soft and filmy with the lingering sensation.

Again that dazzling, blinding smile. Again the tightness in her chest.

'Another time,' he said with great gentleness. 'Believe me, our lives are connected. That's why we are both here. Brace yourself for a shock. It is good news—something life-changing.'

CHAPTER TWO

SOPHIA gulped and sat back in her seat, her mind reeling. She didn't want her life changed. Not drastically, anyway. A job, a man to love and even one child instead of four would do very nicely.

Rozzano's grasp on her hands reassured her. She could feel his strength pouring into her body. Searching the two men's faces, she saw compassion and joy in their expressions. It wouldn't be anything bad, she decided, or they'd be offering her brandy and sympathy and pushing smelling salts under her nose.

'I'm braced,' she said with resignation. 'So tell me.'

The solicitor gestured for Rozzano to continue. The prince studied her with close attention as if he was reading every line of her face. But his expression remained inscrutable. She realised this was a shrewd man, who saw much and revealed little.

'Your mother died when you were...?'

'Two.' Was this relevant? she wondered. But he seemed to be waiting for her to continue, so she decided to humour him. 'She was walking in the village with me in my buggy when a lorry got out of control and...'

She drew her brows together sharply, the slaty depths of her eyes reflecting her emotions. Her father had been inconsolable. She remembered his endless sobbing which had filled the house for days, the hushed parishioners who'd cared for her and her own confusion when her father kept holding her too tightly, making her cry too.

'Poor Father,' she said gently. 'He loved her so much.'

There was a silence in the room. She was glad that Rozzano didn't offer any platitudes or sympathy for people he'd never known.

The warmth of his strong hands seemed to increase. Sophia felt her gaze drawn back to his. 'Tell me about her.'

'I don't remember much,' she confessed. 'I just have an overall impression of hugs and kisses and laughter… Oh, she always smelt wonderful; she had these fabulous bottles of perfume—' She stopped to recover her normal speaking voice.

'Ah. Perfume.' Rozzano's brilliant eyes seemed to be having a hypnotic effect on her.

Sophia drew herself upright, banishing the strange feeling that her body ran with a warm and heavy fluid. Ludicrous. There were definitely bones in there somewhere.

'There are several photos of her in the house of course,' she finished abruptly.

'Would you describe her for me?' the prince asked softly.

She hoped they'd get to the point soon. Her nerves were shredding with every second.

'Tall, slender, long, silky raven hair, merry eyes. And very, very beautiful in a kind of delicate, ethereal way,' she replied, her expression growing wistful.

If only she'd known her mother! She'd lain awake for hours some nights, imagining what it must be like to be one of the other girls in the village, borrowing their mother's make-up, going on shopping trips to town together, coming home from school to the smell of freshly baked cakes…

'Sophia?' prompted the prince. 'Drifting again?'

She nodded and gave him an apologetic look but he

didn't seem to mind. 'I was indulging in wishful thinking. She sounded adorable. Father talked about her a lot. It seemed,' she mused, 'that he felt she'd needed protecting, that she was fragile and vulnerable. Look, I have a picture of her in my bag.'

Rozzano released her hands and she fumbled for the dog-eared and faded snapshot, which had been lovingly examined a thousand times over the years. He took it, nodded and passed it to Frank.

'Violetta D'Antiga, without any shadow of doubt.' Rozzano raised an elegant hand to stop the denial on her lips. 'I've seen a painting of her, Sophia. There's no doubt. D'Antiga was her name before she married.' He paused. 'Your mother originally came from Venice.'

Sophia stared wide-eyed with amazement, her heart thumping as she took this in. So this was the mystery! 'Truly?' she asked shakily.

'Truly,' came Frank's confirmation. 'There's ample proof I can show you.'

For a while she sat there, trying to absorb the news, persuaded only by the certainty in Frank's voice. 'I had...no idea,' she said weakly.

She stared at the prince, who seemed delighted, and she found herself hesitantly smiling too. Then he rose and went to stand by the window. It was as if he knew she needed time to take in what he'd said.

'I'm half-Italian,' she said into the silence.

She heard the clink of cups as the men busied themselves with their coffee. Half-Italian. Images from films and travel programmes came into her head. Sunshine, coffee at little tables in exquisite squares beneath striped awnings, excitable chatter, hands gesticulating theatrically... Rich red wine, loving families and passionate emotions.

Yes. *Yes*! Slowly several things began to click into place and as she chewed the news over she began to understand what made her tick at last.

It had seemed that her emotions had always been at odds with her loving, but almost Victorian, upbringing. It had been so very hard for her to please her beloved father and *not* to dance along the street for joy, not to fling her arms around people and touch them so much, not to gesticulate wildly or laugh and sing and shout with glee whenever she felt happy and glad to be alive...

But this exuberance had been part of her nature. A delighted grin widened her generous mouth.

'Venice!' she said softly. A deep happiness shone in her eyes and she couldn't keep the joy from showing in every line of her animated face. 'Venice!' she whispered with fervent rapture, thinking of the blue lagoon, the islands, the wonderful medieval city built on water...

'You're...pleased?'

Rozzano was leaning casually against the windowsill, but the tautness of his folded arms and the rigidity of his shoulders told a different story. So did the deep throb of his voice. It seemed that her answer was important to him and she found this utterly fascinating.

There was more to come; she knew it. Things they hadn't told her yet. She soberly masked her nervous excitement, forced her hands to relax and replied quite calmly.

'I'm thrilled,' she said in all truth.

'What do you know about Venice?'

Sophia's eyes instantly reflected her dreams. There was a book of the city at home with wonderful photographs... She gave a little laugh, realising now why her father had shown it to her with such care.

'Father stayed there as a young man when he was

training for the church and researching St Mark, for his thesis.' Her face became wreathed in smiles. 'I suppose that's where he met Mother!' she declared sentimentally, imagining the two of them being serenaded in a gondola at midnight, floating silently along the dark canals...

'Sophia? Come back to us?'

The prince's soft and humour-laden murmur brought her back to the present with a jolt. 'I was thinking what a romantic city it must be for lovers,' she explained a little bashfully, adoring the thought of her parents in such a setting. How wonderful it must have been!

'You know it? You've been there?' he asked with interest.

'Oh, no! But Father talked about it and I feel I know it. We'd look at a travel book of the city together and he'd tell me about the *palazzos*, St Mark's Square, the churches crammed full of paintings by famous artists... I feel I know it. I have the map of the island in my head, how the Grand Canal curves like a backward 'S' bend, where the Rialto Bridge is... And it's so beautiful. To me, Venice looks as if it's the backdrop in a medieval fairy tale.'

'It was, once. And I agree. It's the most beautiful city in the world,' Rozzano murmured. 'Venetians feel sorry for anyone not born there!'

'Now what tells me that you're Venetian yourself?' she asked drily. His eyes twinkled at her. Fascinated to learn about her mother's birthplace, she added, 'Have your family lived there long?'

'About seven hundred years,' he replied without any hint of arrogance.

'*Seven...!*' Open-mouthed in amazement, she gave up trying to imagine what it must be like to trace your ancestors so far back and decided to tease him. 'Dear, dear.

And still stuck in Venice!' she chided. 'Not the kind of people to go off and colonise the world, then!'

He threw back his head and laughed in delight before coming forward to take her hands in his. Extraordinary! He kept touching her. Why?

Staring into her startled eyes, he kissed the fingers of both hands. 'When you find a jewel, you don't swap it for paste.'

She lowered her lashes, frowning. The touch of his lips had been warm and soft and she'd wished... Ashamed by her waywardness, she did her best to keep her fingers limp and unresponsive beneath his and searched for the threads of the conversation, bending her mind to getting the loose ends tied up.

'I still don't understand why you're here,' she said, suddenly crisp and efficient. 'And why didn't Father tell me who my mother was? Being Italian isn't a crime. It doesn't make sense.'

The hands holding hers tightened a fraction. 'I imagine he was protecting her.'

Sophia stiffened at the gravity in Rozzano's voice. She'd been right. There was more. Something she wouldn't like. 'Why?' she asked, feeling the fear clutch at her heart and squeeze it hard.

He was watching her like a hawk. 'She had run away.'

Her eyes widened in shock. 'From what?'

'Marriage.'

Absently his thumbs stroked her long fingers and she had to work hard to keep her breathing steady. 'Go on,' she mumbled.

'There had been an understanding that she would marry a family friend when she reached eighteen. She'd been virtually betrothed since childhood. I understand, however, that she was very independent and emotional.

For most of her teenage years she fought against a love-less marriage.'

'So would I!' Sophia declared fervently, feeling appalled at the family pressure her beleaguered mother must have endured.

'Ye-e-s.'

A faint frown drew Rozzano's brows together as if her remark was not to his liking. Abruptly he dropped her hands and began to stroll around the room again, picking up objects absently and putting them down. Sophia and Frank followed his every move and she realised just how dominant the prince was, how he had taken over the situation to make it run at his pace, his discretion.

He was used to taking charge, to being obeyed. Sophia found that both attractive and challenging. Wryly she recognised that she wanted him to know that she wasn't to be ordered around, however mild and compliant she might seem to an outsider. She was her mother's daughter. If anyone pushed her too far, she'd dig her heels in. And it was time she showed that she was the equal of any prince.

'So she married my father for love and defied her materialistic family. Quite right, too. I admire her strength of will. No one should be pushed into an arranged marriage against his or her wishes!'

He gave a very Italian shrug of his tailored shoulders. 'A dynastic marriage is not unusual in my experience. Often an aristocrat's child may grow up with an understanding that he or she will marry someone from a suitable family.'

She wrinkled her nose in disapproval and wondered about Rozzano's wife—because he'd surely be married. He wore a signet ring on the third finger of his left hand, one with diamond shoulders and entwined initials. Would his marriage have been arranged?

She imagined the awkwardness of his wedding night, facing a bride he didn't love. And she blushed when her thoughts took her further as she imagined his broad shoulders and muscular torso naked...

'Barbaric!' she declared with more force than she'd intended. But she felt annoyed that her body was hot with shocking thoughts of gold-skinned nudity... She swallowed. She must stick to the point. 'OK. So what's your connection with her?' she asked, trying to equate this aristocrat and his unnerving pedigree with her own ordinary family.

There was a long pause. Sophia thought she would break the habit of a lifetime and scream. Her lips parted in breathless panic.

'For heaven's sake tell me!' she urged, her voice throbbing with low and intense passion.

Rozzano's liquid eyes seemed unnaturally intent on hers, as if he could see the havoc in her mind. 'Your mother, Violetta, was the daughter of my father's great friend Alberto D'Antiga. She was to be my father's bride. But she jilted him.'

She wondered curiously if Rozzano felt insulted on behalf of his father. He gave no hint of it. On the contrary, she thought, her skin prickling with sensation, he was leaning elegantly against Frank's desk and looking her up and down as if he was giving marks out of ten for every inch she possessed. And the muscles in her body grew tense in response as she battled to stop herself melting into the chair.

He'd be used to that kind of response, she thought crossly, and made sure that he suspected nothing. With a scowl, she said flatly, 'That doesn't explain why you're here.'

The dark eyes became veiled and she wondered if she'd been imagining his appraisal. 'I look after Alberto D'Antiga's affairs. We have old family connections and he is ill and alone in the world,' Rozzano said, a surprising tenderness creeping into his voice. 'Your grandfather is growing weaker every day, Sophia. He will be delighted to know he has a granddaughter.'

'Hmm. This is the man who drove my mother away from the home she loved!' Sophia reminded him vigorously.

'You feel nothing for an old and sick man who is your blood relation?' Rozzano's reproachful glance was putting her to shame.

She heaved a sigh and came off her high horse. 'Of course I do. What's past is past. I'm sorry he's not well. And yes, I'd like to contact him. He's the only family I have now.' Efficiently she whipped a pen and small notebook from her handbag. 'Can you let me have his address?'

'Certainly. Il Conte D'Antiga; that's D apostrophe, capital A...'

'Il Conte...' She looked up to see if the prince was teasing her but he appeared to be perfectly serious.

'His *palazzo* is called Ca' D'Antiga,' he drawled. 'Capital C—'

'Just a minute!' Shock widened her smoke-dark eyes. 'A...count? In a *palace*? You're having me on, aren't you?' she said with a nervous laugh.

'No. He is, as you say, a count.' He saw her disbelief and added quietly, 'There are many *palazzi* in Venice. A few hundred. And there are many minor nobles. We still keep our titles, even after Napoleon abolished them.

Sophia, I would not lie about this. What would be my motive? Think about it. Surely you don't imagine that D'Antiga would have been so anxious about his daughter's marriage if he were a butcher or a gondolier, or perhaps an ice-cream seller?'

'I—I don't know!' she mumbled, unable to take in what he was saying. It made horrible sense suddenly. 'I s-suppose,' she said slowly, leaping to a conclusion that made sense to her and stumbling over her words, 'he was desperate. He'd lost his money and needed his daughter to marry someone rich to preserve—'

'He's wealthy. Always has been.'

With her idea shot down in flames, she shook her head slightly to clear the confusion there. 'Then why did he insist on this loveless marriage?'

'You have to be careful of fortune hunters,' Rozzano said abruptly. 'If wealth marries wealth, the partners are equal.'

Sophia let her horror show. 'No wonder Mother ran away if that's the way you aristocrats think!' she said indignantly, putting the notebook firmly away. 'Love is the only reason for marriage! Anything else would make a mockery of marriage vows taken before God! I'm proud that she valued love more than money—'

'She could have had both.' The prince smiled a little wryly at her raised eyebrows and spoke slowly and with emphasis as if aware that her fuddled brain was working at a snail's pace. 'Your mother was an heiress with a fortune of her own.'

Silence. Stunned by his claim, she stared at him, frowning. That couldn't be right. They'd been horribly poor. They'd shivered in the draughty vicarage and worn extra jumpers and socks against the cold. If there *had* been money, it had long since gone.

She tried to speak, to tell them this, but the words wouldn't come.

Rozzano had moved closer and was now standing over her. She had to look up to see his face, her eyes skittering nervously over his superb body.

Was he deliberately dominating her? she wondered. She contemplated jumping up and doing a bit of striding around herself, but she knew that right at this moment her legs would buckle. A weak, rubbery goo seemed to have replaced her bones.

He pushed back his jacket and thrust his hands into his pockets, drawing her unwilling attention to his narrow waist and slim hips. She lowered her eyes. He was speaking and his purring voice curled into her with remorseless insistence, distracting her even from the staggering claim he'd made about her mother.

He is unbelievably magnetic, she thought, terrified that he'd realise—rightly—that her shallow breathing wasn't entirely due to his revelations. Desperately she struggled to stop herself reacting so stupidly to Rozzano's high-octane sex appeal and to attend to what he was saying.

'But you'll find that your grandfather,' he was telling her smoothly, 'is a kind and generous man. He would be very happy to see you take your place in Venetian society.'

She gave a short laugh, seeing herself parading in a tiara and ermine-trimmed robes, or whatever count's granddaughters wore. Probably fluorescent Versace and a baseball cap nowadays, she thought ruefully, trying to make herself see the funny side.

Rozzano frowned faintly at her scathing expression. 'You're amused?'

'No. Yes. I'm sorry. But it's so *crazy*! I apologise if my reaction has offended you. It's just that I think you should check your facts. Far from being an heiress, my mother was impoverished.'

'How do you know?'

She gave him a pitying glance. 'Because of the way we lived. I know she adored us. She would have shared her money with us, then left it to Father. But he and I lived from hand to mouth! He never had a bean. Look at me! Look at these clothes! They hardly shout "Heiress!", do they? They come from the local nearly new shop!'

She cast a realistic glance at herself. It wasn't surprising that he'd been riveted by her appearance. Having compared her to the photo of Violetta D'Antiga, he would have begun to wonder how Violetta could have given birth to such a poorly dressed shambles of a woman!

'All I know is that she didn't touch her trust fund. It's still intact in a Venetian bank,' Rozzano said relentlessly.

'But...why would she do that, deliberately make herself poor?' Sophia demanded in disbelief.

'Pride and fear,' answered Frank. 'Violetta's father was—is—one of the trustees. She would have had to ask him to release the money. From what your father said, I gather she felt her happiness would have been compromised by wealth—something she didn't want to risk. I had the whole story from your father; it's in this letter.' He held it out to her.

'I can't believe that!' she cried vehemently, desperate to deny it all, afraid of the doubts crowding her mind, afraid there might be some truth in this preposterous story.

Suddenly she felt very scared, as if the ground had been swept from under her to leave a gaping hole beneath. And she was falling into it, like it or not.

Words spun around her mind. Italian. Venice. A count. An heiress. Obviously she'd fallen asleep by the window in Frank's waiting room and this was a dream, prompted by thinking of the prince. She drove her top teeth into her lower lip.

And knew she was awake.

Shaking, she clapped a hand to her forehead. It burned, yet her cheek felt clammy. A fever. Hallucinations, then.

'Please... ' she whispered, feeling hot and unbearably dizzy. 'I—I can't breathe...'

Strong arms enfolded her, one slipping around her back, one tucking beneath her knees. He'd done this before, she thought muzzily, and pouted, irrationally resenting all the women he'd carried to bed. Her head swam as she was raised in the air as if she weighed nothing.

Nauseous, with the room seeming to whirl about her, she allowed herself to be borne a short distance to an old sofa by the window, where Rozzano gently laid her.

Her eyes closed as she fought the swirling mist filling her head. She mustn't pass out. She had to focus her mind, deal with this mad suggestion... And yet Frank had been so certain. It couldn't be true...could it?

A moan whispered through her pale lips. The evidence was overwhelming. Why else had the prince come to England? The facts were staring her in the face. Frank was convinced. So was the prince. That meant... She groaned, then shuddered when Rozzano whispered something to her and his fingers lightly smoothed her furrowed brow.

'Water, please!' he called urgently.

Warm silk touched her chin. A jacket lining, she thought hazily, as its weight settled across her body. It smelled of him, a fragrance that was faint and elusive but wonderfully enticing, like the natural perfumes her mother had used. And she wanted to reach up her arms and pull him down to her till his cheek rested against hers and she could inhale those delicious scents.

Instead she kept her eyes tightly shut, giving herself thinking space. And time to settle her wild and shocking urges. Something awful had happened to her. The news had weakened her, torn her apart and left her defences open to the first devastatingly handsome man who crossed her path. And Rozzano was more devastating and handsome than most.

'Goodness!' exclaimed the temp, tapping in on her tottery heels.

Sophia blessed the woman for ripping into her panic-stricken thoughts. Nevertheless, she remained still, listening to Frank's muttered dismissal. Cool water was being dabbed on her temples and wrists.

And then Rozzano's moistened finger brushed a few times across her trembling mouth. It was terribly, wonderfully sexy and she didn't know how she kept her eyes shut or stopped herself from catching his fingertip between her lips and tasting it, perhaps letting it wander into the moistness of her mouth...

At the contraction of her loins, Sophia moaned again, aware she needed to release her deep and terrifying feelings. She was in a state of turmoil, and no wonder. Desperately she gritted her teeth, appalled at the way her barriers were tumbling.

His hand stroked hers rhythmically—she knew it was his, recalled its strength, the sinews, the dryness of his palms and the suppleness of his long fingers. And she realised that she could also recall every line of his face, the angles of his eyebrows, the way he stood, walked...

'Sophia, just relax,' he murmured somewhere near her ear.

Relax! Suppressing a sharp gasp when his cool breath feathered over her face, she went through every muscle of her body, one by one, in an attempt to do as he said.

She opened her eyes and wished she hadn't. He was leaning over her, kiss-close, an expression of concern softening his autocratic features.

'Don't be alarmed,' he said. 'Nothing bad will come of this, Sophia. You and your grandfather will be re-united. You won't have to worry about money ever again—'

'My grandfather!' she breathed raggedly, feeling emotion sweep over her.

She was too choked to continue. All these years and the old man had aged and become ill, unaware that she existed. Without any warning, she began to cry as she lay there, the hot tears squeezing themselves pathetically from the corners of her eyes and running down her cheeks to the top of her jaw.

'Why's she upset?' she heard Frank hiss. 'I thought she'd be pleased! She deserves a break after all she's been through,' he said, warming to his theme while Sophia cringed with dismay at being openly discussed. 'She gave up everything to look after her father. It can't have been easy. No fun, no boyfriends, all those years of devoted attention—'

'Frank,' she mumbled hastily before the violins started playing, 'you don't understand! I'm crying because I have a grandfather who doesn't even know I'm alive. He might have died and I would never have met him! How could my mother have done this to me?' she cried passionately, so distressed that she forgot her reserve. 'Why did she keep me from her family? She was married. She would have been beyond her father's interference! Surely they could have made up their differences! It seems so cruel—' She faltered, her eyes filling with tears again. 'My mother's become a mystery. I hate that,' she finished miserably.

'Then find out. Come to Venice and talk to your grandfather,' suggested Rozzano gently. 'Let him explain.'

'Venice?' she cried in blank amazement, sitting up.

'Of course,' the prince said patiently. 'He can't come to you. He isn't strong. Any day now I fear the worst...'

She bit her lip, getting his drift. Her grandfather didn't have long to live and time was running out. She hesitated. 'I couldn't afford the trip—'

'You can. You're rich,' he reminded her.

'I don't have a passport,' she said stubbornly, blanking her mind to all the things she didn't want to deal with.

And she knew she was clutching at any straw to stop her from making the journey, even though she longed to meet her grandfather. Fear and love were vying with one another.

'No passport?' Rozzano exclaimed in amazement.

'There's never been any need,' she said stiffly. 'My birth certificate was lost and—'

'Not lost. In my safekeeping.' Frank held it out to her.

And there it was. Mother: La Contessa Violetta D'Antiga. Sophia stared at it but her fingers were shaking so much that it fell from her fingers to the floor. Rozzano reached out to retrieve it and as he bent his cheek came so close that it almost brushed hers.

She felt her chest become banded with iron and her breath suck in sharply.

'I know this must be difficult for you, but I'll help

you,' he said, so softly that she strained closer to hear. 'I'll be with you every step of the way if you wish.'

There was a sudden violent movement in the open doorway to the waiting room. Almost simultaneously she was dazzled by a series of blinding flashes which made her scream in fear.

Rozzano shot to his feet, muttering ferociously in Italian under his breath, and in a matter of seconds he was roaring through the door in hot pursuit of the intruder.

Sophia saw Frank move to the window. She jumped up with a sudden surge of energy and joined him. Her heart leapt to her mouth. In the street below, Rozzano was shouting and clinging onto the door of a car, which was accelerating away.

'He'll be killed!' she croaked in horror.

Without thinking, she dashed out of the office and down the stairs, running like the wind after the careering car. Rozzano fell, and rolled away from it.

And lay motionless.

He was deeply shaken, though not by his fall, or the brush with danger. He'd taken too many risks paragliding and skiing and had faced fear too often for it to affect him any more. It was his reaction that staggered him.

Astonishingly, he'd wanted to protect Sophia from press exposure—from the lies, and the stories they'd weave about them both. Her scream of terror had aroused in him a response so visceral and primitive that he might have been a caveman, defending his woman!

And so he'd done the unthinkable, broken his own rules, and acted like a fool. He could have kicked himself. The press would have a field-day with this one.

Furious at his stupidity, he lay without moving, allow-ing his anger to fade and his bruised muscles to recover. He became aware that his head throbbed. A gentle hand touched it. Sophia's. Wonderful.

His body responded immediately, much to his annoyance, generating warmth in his loins. To his astonishment, the heady combination of virgin and siren had fired an almost uncontrollable desire in him, a desire more powerful than anything he'd felt for years.

Her dreamy smile had driven him mad. He'd wanted to know what she was thinking whenever she 'drifted'. And, he wanted to be a part of her fantasies. Dammit! He'd have to get a grip.

She checked his pulse. He felt it falter then accelerate and she murmured in tender concern. And he felt cherished for the first time in his life.

Guilt crawled all through him. She was so honest and trusting. He knew he shouldn't lie there inert—but the urge to play patient to her nurse was overwhelming. Even the thought of that scenario brought a skin-tingling frisson curling through his every nerve, tightening every sinew and heating his blood.

He knew why he'd reacted so violently. The opportunity for action had seemed almost welcome and it had released some of the exquisite agony which had been building up in his love-starved body.

He could smell her now. Wanted to lift his face and inhale her intoxicating fragrance. Disgusted with his lack of control, he pressed his hands harder into the ground and let the gravel take his mind off his carnal needs.

But it was a struggle. Her hands were now systematically feeling his limbs for breakages and he all but groaned, the warmth in his loins becoming searing hot. Desperate to curb any physical reaction to the electric sensation of her hands on his body, he concentrated doggedly on the sounds of the small crowd gathering around them.

They knew her. Liked her. Felt concern for her. He could hear the love in their voices and he was glad. Such a good and decent woman would bring delight to frail Alberto D'Antiga's soft heart and the old man would die in peace, knowing that his family name was in good hands.

Unless, of course, some good-looking, gold-digging parasite turned her head! His brows drew together moodily. That mustn't happen. She'd be hurt. Or worse... corrupted. His jaw tightened. He was back in caveman mode again, taking up his cudgel to crack the head of any man who harmed her. Was that the reaction Violetta had prompted in men?

'He's in pain!' she cried.

He felt the light touch of Sophia's fingers on his forehead smoothing out the frown lines and heard her soft murmur as she spoke to him, pleading with him, an appealing little catch in her voice giving him immense problems with his self-control.

'Please open your eyes!' she begged.

'Now don' thee be upsettin' theself,' came a deep, Dorset voice above him.

Warmth and caring flooded to the distressed Sophia. She was clearly a much loved and exceptional woman. It confirmed his initial assessment that Violetta's daughter was a woman in a million, imbued with rare qualities...

No wonder he'd been intrigued by her. Had wanted to make love to her, then and there! How he'd stopped himself he didn't know. It was like being a teenager again, ruled by sudden unbridled lust!

And it unnerved him because he wouldn't be able to

walk away from her unwelcome attractions. He'd have to be with her, hour after hour, day after day, introducing her to Venetian society, worrying about her innocence...

He stopped breathing. Something had occurred to him and his brain went into overdrive. Sophia's hand lay on his chest and she was beginning to panic at its lack of movement, so he let his breath out slowly. He had the answer to all his problems. And as she relaxed in relief he neatly fitted her into his momentous decision.

He would marry her.

CHAPTER THREE

IT WAS a brilliant solution, he thought. A strange, breathless excitement stole over him. He didn't love her—never could love any woman. But she would make the perfect wife.

Her hands had moved to his upper thigh. They trembled as she tested the movement of his femur. It was obvious from her hesitant touch that she knew little of men. A surge of excitement almost betrayed him as he imagined teaching her the pleasures of the flesh.

His breathing rasped harshly. He could hardly wait. Sophia even had money of her own! Too many title-seekers and materialistic women had propositioned him. But Sophia…she was different. She had values he admired. She had an eagerness to work and concern for others. She had nursed her ailing father and, more important, she adored children.

Children. He bucked as a shaft of pain sliced through him when the nightmare memory forced its way to the surface. Her hand rested gently on his chest and thinking of her sweet face helped him to drive the dark hell away again.

'He may have cracked a rib,' she said anxiously. 'Did you see how his chest contracted then?'

Racked with guilt, he suffered the gentle exploration of her hands. The pain was deeper than she knew. Deep enough to shut off his heart for ever. Like his father, he had married into the D'Antiga family. He'd been twenty-eight, and had fallen head over heels for the recently divorced Nicoletta who, unknown to him, had a highly colourful sexual past.

A dainty, extravagant thirty-two, she had worked her wiles on him and stolen his heart. They'd only been married for two years when she'd died, pregnant with his child.

Desperately he pushed back the rest of the horror. He couldn't deal with it, couldn't make it known. If he did, the Barsini name would be vilified.

But Sophia could ease his nightmares. He needed her tenderness. Hope began to surge through him, and for the first time in years he believed he could find some kind of happiness.

And she? He tried to see his intentions from her point of view. She had shown an appealingly bewildered interest in him. The sex would be fantastic. Her passions ran deep, with an intensity that matched his own. He'd read that in her eyes, in every gesture of her highly charged body.

He could make her happy. He *would* make her happy. And he could help her to cope, too. It would be hard for her, he argued, to dive head first into Venetian society without a guide. And who better than him to be her mentor?

'He's still not responding! I think we should call the doctor,' she said anxiously.

'Gone to Durbridge,' came the reply. 'Vet's not far, though. Or the baby nurse'll be along in a minute.'

Rozzano held back a grin. He'd better 'recover' before he experienced some interesting medical practices! Then all he had to do was to win her over—and quickly, before the wolf pack moved in, intent on her money and title. Opening his eyes slowly, he saw the relief on her pale, wide-eyed face.

'You're all right!'

He wanted to take her in his arms and reassure her. And felt a fraud for his deception. 'Shaken,' he said uncomfortably, even though it was the truth.

There was a murmur from the crowd and he was immediately bathed in smiles and friendly words of warning to be careful, to take it easy, to sit up slowly when he felt ready, no rush, don't you fret...

He felt bad and couldn't meet their eyes. Many hands helped him to sit and then stand. Someone brushed dust from his back. Someone else offered to fetch him a brandy from the nearby pub. The local midwife—presumably the baby nurse—anxiously offered her services and he declined with gravity yet with a twinkle in his eyes which set everyone laughing.

And all the time he was thinking of Sophia, planning, scheming, and stemming his eagerness to begin now, this minute, to hold her, kiss her luscious mouth...

At last they were alone. A few yards away, he could hear Luscombe's raised voice and he hoped the temp was getting short shrift. The photo would be dynamite.

'I'm sorry,' he said to Sophia, standing as close as he judged acceptable. The wind blew tendrils of her hair around her face and he caught a tantalising perfume in the air. He forced himself to stay just where he was though he shook in the attempt. 'I tried to stop that photographer but—'

'What was he up to?' she said, weaving loose tendrils of hair into her braid. 'How did he know you were there?'

'I'd say, judging from the argument going on behind us, that Luscombe's secretary was the culprit,' he told her drily. 'I expect she contacted the local photographer when she saw who'd been booked in for the eleven o'clock appointment.'

Sophia shook her head in bewilderment. 'Just because you're a prince?'

He grinned, loving her astonishment. He'd never impress her with his illustrious ancestors! 'Amazing, isn't it? It's possible she switched on Luscombe's intercom when she brought in the coffee and listened in to everything we said. The photographer must have thought it was his birthday when she was called in to bring you a glass of water and found me bending over you.'

Her cheeks flamed. And all the time he was thinking that he had to get her alone to begin his seduction. He could think of several single men who'd adore her. And many married ones—including his brother. He went cold.

'Are you all right?' she asked, tentatively touching his arm.

He nodded, his hand across his face to hide the snarl which wanted to rip across it. 'A twinge. Just a minute and I'll be fine,' he said tightly.

He knew what would happen. Once Enrico knew his plans for Sophia, he'd do everything in his power to make his life hell. Perhaps... He stiffened till his entire body shook with passion. There was no 'perhaps'. Sadly he knew his brother too well.

Enrico would seduce her himself out of sheer spite!

'I think you need a cup of tea,' she said, her hand lightly stroking his back.

Tea! He looked at her helplessly. She'd be eaten alive and spat out by Enrico without a moment's thought. He had to take action—now.

An idea came to him. He called over to Frank. 'I think I should get Sophia away from here,' he told the solicitor, doing his best to look worried.

A pang of guilt nudged his conscience but he pushed it away. The ends justified the means. Sophia needed protection. He dreaded to think what indignities Enrico would put her through before he finished with her.

'That photo will be seen as incriminating,' he went on. He took a step closer and his hands closed around her shoulders. His heart began to thunder. 'It will look as if we were engaged in an intimate moment together.' He wished! The excitement ran like a river through him and he was amazed that she didn't feel its power and slap his face.

She swallowed. 'In...intimate?'

'Think about it. You lying on a sofa, me leaning over you as if I'm about to kiss you—' Which he almost was, he thought wryly.

'But that's not true!'

Her cheeks had deepened to the colour of a rose. So enticing.

'I know that, you know it, but pictures lie. The press makes what it wants of a shot, as I know to my cost. There'll be an intense interest in you. Life will be unbearable. They'll crowd around you, shouting, pushing, thrusting microphones in your face, popping flash bulbs and generally making your every movement impossible.'

He felt her shoulders tense up. Without thinking, he stroked them and her muscles eased beneath his soothing fingers before her gasp of alarm made him stop. But he let his hands remain. He needed to touch her, to feel her warmth, to inhale the freshness of her skin. To dream. To imagine removing her clothes, slowly, tormenting himself exquisitely as he revealed her body beneath.

He wanted her for himself, he realised. Somewhere secret and private where he could quietly begin to make love to her...

'They'll lose interest when I tell them what really happened!' she declared shakily.

She had no idea what lay ahead. He pitied her. She had a lot to learn. 'Fine,' he said, using ruthlessness to get his own way. 'You do that. Tell them that you felt faint because you'd just discovered that your mother was a Venetian heiress. Explain that you're a countess and disgustingly rich. What do you think they'd do with that story? "Jobless girl out for the Count". Or "Rags to riches". The Cinderella story is a fantasy everyone would love to read about. It would run and run.'

She stared at him in horror. He moved closer, drawn by her helplessness. 'I see,' she said unhappily. 'But they'll leave me alone once they know how ordinary I am, surely?'

It came to him then. She was vulnerable. She would need him. That was how he would break down her resistance. He would offer his protection, take charge of her life, and teach her...everything.

Sophia felt safe at last. Here in a suite in the River House Hotel, with Rozzano next door, she would be protected from the nightmare scenarios he had described so graphically on the journey from Dorset to London.

It was Frank who'd convinced her to hide herself among London's teeming millions for a day or so. Sophia had managed to pack a case and seemingly in no time at all she was in Rozzano's Lear jet, curled up in a vast armchair seat. His hair-raising tales about the press had scared her stiff, and she'd hated the fact that she might be chased by the media wherever she went. How could she ever live like a normal person?

'Loosen up, Sophia.' He'd drawn her to him comfortingly. 'All this has been a shock, I know, but give it time. Live each moment, and make plans later. In the meantime, let me handle everything.'

'Thank you,' she muttered weakly.

It occured to her that she'd never been weak before. It must be something to do with being thrown into the deep end of life suddenly. She'd never felt so vulnerable, never needed someone strong and protective until now.

He tightened his hold on her. Now she could feel the hardness of his hipbone, the warmth of his body and its subtle fragrance.

'I can't ever become part of your world,' she said, feeling forlorn.

'You are part of it. In fact, you're very similar to me.'

Sophia was intrigued. 'In what way?'

'Being a vicar's daughter has taught you restraint, courtesy, good manners and concern for others. You will have learnt to put the feelings of other people before your own and concealed your emotions and needs—'

'How did you know that?' she exclaimed in amazement.

Rozzano looked at her gravely. 'That was my upbringing too. I know what it's like to be torn between polite behaviour and the desire to let rip. Society has made demands on us both which we've tried to fulfil. You will fit very well into what you call my world. The goodness of your heart will see you through any social situation you encounter. Everything else is unimportant.'

She remained within the circle of his arms, astonished by the similarities between them and the kindness of his words. It was the sort of wise observation her father would have made—and she'd believed there were few men with as gentle and perceptive a nature as him. Her admiration for Rozzano deepened.

'Don't forget,' Rozzano added more cynically, 'that people will accept you because you're a millionairess.'

'You're kidding!' From the gravity of his expression, it was clear that he wasn't.

A millionairess! She went hot and cold.

'Think what you can do with so much money.' He gave a small, wintry smile. 'A wardrobe or two of gorgeous clothes, shoes, luxurious holidays—'

'Stop! You're testing my puritanical upbringing to the utmost!' Sophia protested, trying not to be seduced by the thought of silk undies and flattering clothes. And someone to tell her what to do with her hair... 'No,' she said firmly, 'I grant you it'll be a joy not to wonder if I can pay my bills, but just think, Rozzano, what I can do! Help people in need, for instance, like...orphans, the homeless, sick children... I've felt frustrated and helpless whenever I've watched TV reports showing human suffering. I've given what I can, but it has always seemed an insignificant amount.' Her eyes sparkled as the power of money hit home. 'I can be much more generous in future. So the media does good as well as bad, Rozzano. We wouldn't hear of these tragedies if they didn't publicise them.'

He grunted. 'Are you always so even-handed?'

'I try to be fair.'

She lowered her lashes, confused by his thoughtful stare. 'And I will try to help you, to be by your side whenever you need me.' His voice was husky, his eyes warm. If she didn't know better, she'd have thought he was flirting. She picked at the wavy hem of her cardigan and saw herself through his eyes—a less than beautiful, unsophisticated woman with metaphorical straw in her hair. Besides, she remembered, he was married. Her hand flew to her mouth as something awful occurred to her.

She groaned aloud. 'Rozzano! That photo! Your wife

will think you...I... She'll be furious! I'm terribly
sorry—'

'My wife is dead, Sophia. This is my family ring,
handed down through the generations. I always wear it.'

Hearing the flatness of his tone, she glanced at him
with quick dismay. A dark anguish had briefly shown in
his eyes before he'd lowered his gaze. But there was a
stony coldness about his face that he couldn't disguise,
and his expressive mouth was thin and drawn.

The penny dropped. It had been his wife's death that
had prompted his despair and which had been shown so
graphically in that photograph she'd seen. And it was
painfully obvious that he'd loved her deeply.

Painful for her, as well as him, it seemed. To her utter
horror, it made her feel miserable that he still mourned
his late wife. She was appalled at herself. What was she
to him? Nothing but a duty, someone to take care of on
behalf of a family friend. She had no *right* to be upset.

Arranged marriage or not, naturally he would have
been able to select the most beautiful, most accom-
plished, most desirable woman around. Who was she to
envy that woman? And yet, to her great shame, she did.

Shaken, she remained silent for the rest of the journey
while Rozzano retreated broodingly into some inner
world she dared not enter.

Now, in her suite next to Rozzano's at the hotel with
its dramatic views of the Thames and the Houses of
Parliament, she showered and changed into a home-made
sleeveless dress. It skimmed her collarbone and fitted
snugly to her body then flared out from the neat waistline.
She instantly felt comfortable in it—until she checked
herself in the long gold gesso mirror.

'Too much bosom, too much leg,' she muttered in dismay. She might as well have written 'come-and-get-me' on her front!

Uneasily she slipped her bare feet into a pair of pale beige sandals with a small heel, knowing she'd packed only a few items and her choice was limited. The sundress would be needed for the next day. Jeans would be an insult. Sophia's nose wrinkled. She couldn't bear to wear the polyester ever again, so she'd have to stay as she was.

For some reason, her plait looked incongruous. Impatiently she unravelled it and brushed her hair, wondering what to do with it. She saw to her surprise how it cascaded about her shoulders in heavy waves, the rich chestnut tones glinting and gleaming in the light of the massive chandelier.

'Very flamboyant. Very Italian,' she said to herself, and smiled weakly.

There was a knock on the interconnecting door and she panicked, dithering for a moment. She knew she ought to screw her hair into a prim braid—and perhaps hide her 'come-and-get-mes' beneath the saggy cardigan. But vanity won that particular battle. Blushing already at her idiotic decision, she whipped her hair up in a hurried heap on top of her head and secured it with a few hasty pins.

Her heart beat hard as she rushed into the sitting room, aware that tendrils of her hair were already escaping and probably making her look a terrible fright.

Panting and flushed, with one hand pushing rebellious bits of hair back into place, she opened the door. Her lips parted involuntarily when she saw him. A pain caught at her breast and she turned away, walking unsteadily into the middle of the room. He'd gone for the casual look:

a pale gold shirt with hip-hugging linen trousers. And he looked absolutely devastating.

Panic set in. When he'd suggested that it would be safer to eat in her suite, she'd agreed. Too late, she realised that she'd committed herself to an evening with an incredibly sexy male.

'You look…beautiful.'

She stiffened, her back still to him. She looked *better* than when he'd last seen her, but hardly beautiful, with hanks of hair flopping down at all angles. He didn't have to be patronising.

'Thank you,' she said in stilted tones, raising both arms and frantically fiddling with pins. She heard his indrawn breath. Exasperation, she assumed. His normal dinner companions would be groomed to the last eyelash.

'Do you have everything you need?' he asked politely.

No. I need to be gorgeous. A dainty size ten, with enormous brown eyes and a two-year stint at a finishing school in Geneva. A low-cut slinky gown in emerald silk would be nice, too. She grinned, her sense of humour popping up again and enabling her to face him.

'At the last count, I had ninety-five fluffy white towels, two soft and fluffy bathrobes, enough bath gels to wash the entire nation, various shoe cleaning and sewing kits— and probably a set of spanners, for all I know!'

He laughed at her exaggerations and then she remembered her manners. 'You've been very kind to me,' she said shyly. 'Thank you. I really appreciate all the time and trouble you've gone to.'

A flicker of light sliced across his eyes and then was gone. 'It's not a chore. I've enjoyed myself.' He smiled, his teeth a brilliant white as he went on cheerfully, 'We got up here just in time. The manager tells me that the foyer is seething with journalists and photographers.'

Sophia stared, appalled. 'But…how can we ever go out?'

He looked at her steadily, then arranged himself with a certain smugness in an armchair. 'We don't.'

'You can't be serious!' she cried. 'Are you suggesting we stay holed up here like rats in a trap——?'

'Some rats. Some trap,' he murmured, waving a graceful hand at the gorgeous furnishings. 'We could always look for those spanners and practise a bit of DIY and force an escape route.'

She glared. 'It's not funny, Rozzano! I'm used to walking a few miles a day! I need to go out, to breathe fresh air! I can't stay indoors indefinitely just because a bunch of journalists are sniffing around! I don't believe this!' she said, her voice wobbling as she fought angry tears and the urge to stamp her foot petulantly. 'I want out! I don't want to be a countess, I don't want to be wealthy and I want to go home!'

'I'm afraid,' he said quietly, 'that will make an even better story. "Heiress's daughter rejects millions". "Barefoot Contessa chooses sleepy Dorset". You're on the rollercoaster now, Sophia. You can't get off. Think of your grandfather.'

Her face fell. 'You're right. I can't turn my back on him. What can we do?'

There was a knock on the door. 'I'll think of something,' he promised with annoying cheerfulness, rising to open it.

A waiter wheeled in a trolley, bade them both good evening and began to transfer linen, cutlery and glasses to the dining table by the window whilst exchanging pleasantries.

'Thank you.' Rozzano held out a large tip and glanced at the waiter's name badge. 'You've seen nothing, heard nothing, Tony, OK? I might need you again. I want to know I can rely on your discretion if there's trouble with the press.'

The money slipped into the waiter's top pocket with the speed of lightning. 'I'm blind, deaf and dumb, with an appalling memory, sir,' he said with a grin. 'Goodnight.'

The strain of the day suddenly became too much and tears began to wash into Sophia's eyes. 'I hate being pursued, Rozzano!' she said brokenly, giving way to her misery and sobbing pathetically.

In concern, he moved towards her, and for one glorious moment or two he held her close. Her wet lashes lifted and she gazed at him with big, soulful eyes. As she quivered in his arms for those brief, beautiful few seconds, she felt a lurch of her heart.

And knew she could all too easily fall in love with him.

'Morning, Sophia.'

Smelling delicious, and looking incredibly handsome in a honey and cream striped shirt, toffee-coloured trousers and a toning tie, he greeted her in the continental way—bestowing three kisses on her cheeks.

His cool fingers lightly touched the strap of her sprigged dress and accidentally strayed to her collarbone. Sophia jerked away, startled by the contrast of her burning skin. Eating in the privacy of her suite was turning out to be more dangerous than braving the media downstairs.

'Croissants!' he exclaimed, seeing the breakfast trolley. 'One of my weaknesses,' he enthused. 'No problem with breakfast arriving? No paparazzi leaping from the trolley?' he enquired, as they sat down to eat.

'None that I noticed!'

'Good. My strategy is working. I arranged for a couple of heavies to patrol the corridor,' he said with satisfaction.

'Heavies!' she marvelled, thinking she'd be one soon, if she ate this breakfast in its entirety. 'How the other half lives!'

'It's just temporary,' he said with light-hearted casualness. 'The media will get bored with us soon. So,' he went on, gallantly pretending great interest, 'how did you sleep?'

'Terribly.' Feeling spaced out from her disturbed night, she poured coffee for them both.

Concentrating hard on showing him she could speak and act at the same time, she put far too much sugar in her coffee. She groaned. At this rate, she'd grow enormous!

His dark, beautiful eyes simmered at her over the rim of his glass of juice. 'You should have woken me,' he reproached her.

Sophia was shocked but imagined herself doing just that, slinking in wearing her washed-out, up-to-the-neck nightie. Did he wear pyjamas? Black silk? Or…nothing? She felt her face grow hot and looked down quickly to distract herself by chasing a stubborn mushroom around her plate.

Grimly she fought for control of her body, which was still responding waywardly to the image of Rozzano, naked beneath a pure linen sheet. Her throat was as dry as sawdust. She took a hasty gulp of coffee and choked on the scalding liquid. Waving him back to his seat when he half rose to help her, she drank down her freshly squeezed orange juice and scrabbled for the remnants of her dignity.

'So what was the problem that kept you awake?' he asked genially, as if he hadn't noticed her stupid gaucheries.

She couldn't answer that. The previous evening he'd been very attentive. She'd talked about her life and he'd spoken eloquently about the D'Antiga family perfume business and passionately about Venice, painting a picture so appealing and romantic that her fears had begun to vanish.

They'd laughed a lot. He'd been polite enough to flirt. And then, when they'd bade one another goodnight, he'd hesitated at the interconnecting door, swung around and kissed her gently and lingeringly on each cheek, leaving her trembling and weak at the knees.

Sleep? No wonder she had hardly managed a wink! She heaved an inner sigh. 'I had a lot to think about,' she fudged.

'And? You will come to Venice, won't you?' he said, catching her hand persuasively. 'Your grandfather will be so excited to see you. And I would be delighted to show you around my city.'

She couldn't tear her eyes away from his. Oh, yes! she thought longingly. But it would be a painful pleasure. He'd rattle on about the sights and she'd be wishing his interest in her were more than a friendly, generous duty.

'Some day,' she said slowly, extricating her hand.

'Then let me arrange a passport for you. I can get one quickly.'

'You'd have to run the gauntlet of photographers first,' she reminded him. 'I swear that someone's been in the corridor all night, snuffling and shuffling around like a truffle-hunting pig! It's unbelievable, the lengths these people will go to!' she muttered indignantly, hacking vi-

ciously into a perfectly innocent and defenceless herb
sausage.

He smiled, watching her in amusement. 'You'll get
used to it,' he said airily. 'Although it would be different
in Venice. I can control what happens there more easily.'

She wouldn't get used to it, ever. 'I need to get out
today,' she said abruptly. 'I need fresh air! I feel like a
prisoner!' she declared dramatically.

Amazed at the change in herself—when had she ever
been a drama queen before?—she jumped up and strode
to the window, only to discover that it didn't open.

'Double-glazing. Keeps out the sound of traffic. Shall
I turn on the air conditioning?' came Rozzano's smooth
voice just an inch behind her.

Her skin seemed to tighten. She stared out. Milling
about far below was a posse of photographers with step-
ladders, and a number of journalists, smoking and chatting and looking bored.

'Look at them waiting to pounce! We'll have to use
the back entrance to the hotel,' she said crossly.

'They're old hands at this, Sophia. The back will be
covered too,' he said lazily. His mobile phone began to
trill and he pulled it from its holster, moving away
slightly—much to her relief. 'Excuse me... *Pronto*,
Barsini...'

There was a long silence. The hairs on Sophia's neck
prickled. Rozzano had stiffened and she could see that
he was incandescent with rage—but controlling it, his
voice barely betraying his real feelings as he spoke in
measured tones in his native language.

It was Enrico, taunting him about Sophia. Apparently
their story was splashed across the local rag on the lines
of 'Prince of Sorrow finds joy at last'.

And Enrico was fascinated. 'What *were* you doing, Zano?' he gibed. 'It's not like you to leap on a woman!'

'She fainted when she heard who she was,' he answered laconically. 'I was trying to bring her round. Shock, I think. Not surprisingly, she's overwhelmed.'

'I can't wait to meet her,' Enrico purred. 'Pity the photo was so poor—I couldn't make her out clearly. Do you think,' he added slyly in words meant to wound, 'I'll get on with her as well as I did with Nicoletta?'

He couldn't breathe for a moment. Livid with rage, he forced his teeth together so that no betraying explosion would confirm his brother's suspicions about Sophia. With every ounce of his being he longed to threaten Enrico, to say that if he harmed Sophia—as he'd harmed Nicoletta—then he'd wish he'd never been born. But that kind of reaction would only fire Enrico up.

'Don't get your hopes up. She's an English horse,' he lied, striding around the room to loose off excess energy. 'Tall, big, awkward. Knocks things over.' He scooped up a sneer from somewhere. 'Touch her and she'll neigh with fear.'

'Is she a virgin?' Enrico asked, with a coarse laugh.

He'd swing for his brother one day! 'How the devil would I know? She's weird, I know that. Doesn't know the first thing about etiquette and her clothes are appalling!' he scathed. And he hated himself for distorting the truth. 'I must go, Enrico,' he said quickly. 'Someone's at the door. Speak to you later.'

He was shaking. Although he'd cut the call, he kept the phone to his ear, trying to avoid speaking to Sophia for a few moments. He wasn't in control of himself yet. Fury blazed beneath his lowered lids as he pretended to murmur sporadically into his mobile. He became aware that he was gripping it so hard that the whites of his knuckles showed, and he forced himself to ease up and to pace his breathing.

Think. He had to think. He knew his brother too well, knew how bored he was, how eagerly he grasped any chance for amusement. He glared at the wall, almost overwhelmed by the urge to drive his fist hard into it.

Enrico would make it his business to charm Sophia at the first opportunity. Women seemed to fall for his little-boy-lost look. Why should Sophia be any different?

Rozzano knew that he'd have to take any opportunity to seduce her. She must be his even before they reached Venice.

A whirlwind seduction. No holds barred. He glanced over at the anxious-looking Sophia and he felt his heart pound.

CHAPTER FOUR

'MY BROTHER,' he said tautly, putting his phone away.
'Enrico. Apparently we're front-page news in Venice.
And here, too, I wouldn't wonder. My press office will
issue a total denial of our relationship at home and
threaten to sue. I can't do anything here, I'm afraid.'

Sophia gasped, her hand going to her mouth in horror.
She wouldn't cope with a full-scale press onslaught, he
thought.

Granite-faced, he called Room Service and asked for
Tony to bring him a copy of every paper. When Tony
arrived he grimly handed the waiter the 'Do Not Disturb'
notice to be hung on the door.

The tabloids had their pictures plastered all over their
front pages. They'd gone for 'Prince and the Pauper' as
their angle. The name Cinderella cropped up a few times.
He felt angry that Frank's temp had released Sophia's
story. The woman could be seen simpering from several
centre pages with her skirt hitched up, her body bent
forward to display her cleavage.

'Astonishing—some of the facts are true,' he observed
cynically.

'Lies are mixed up with truths. How can anyone separate one from the other?' she wailed.

'It's how they work,' he said quietly.

He read on. Every article referred back to his wife's
tragic death. And how his wife had been pregnant. He
didn't want to think about that now. It was in the past.
And best left there. He sat there, absorbing every word

in a zombie-like stillness, his face set like marble while she grew more and more agitated beside him.

Suddenly he feared that he wouldn't be able to win Sophia over. The time-scale was too brief. He'd fail—and she would fall into Enrico's hands like a ripe plum. He covered his face with his hands, unable to bear the thought of his brother ruining such an innocent and trusting woman.

'This must be awful for you, Rozzano!' she said in a low, choked voice. 'All this about your wife...'

Tight-lipped, unable to speak or stay for the searing anger and bitterness in his heart, he rose and walked stiffly to the connecting door, gesturing with his hand in wordless apology for his abrupt departure.

'I can't bear to see you so unhappy!' she cried huskily as if she really did feel his pain.

That made it worse. He had to stop in his tracks—or risk stumbling like a drunk—because his mind was full of conflicting thoughts and his eyes seemed to be blurred.

Tentative fingers touched his back and he flinched, afraid that he might lose control completely and blurt out to her that his brother was evil, that it amused him to hurt others. And he might tell her that she was in danger if she didn't put herself under his protection. Even then, she'd have to stay with him all the time...

'Forgive me,' she said. 'I shouldn't have touched you like that. I only... I wanted to apologise.'

'You? Apologise?' he queried, emotion roughening his voice.

'It's because of me all this has happened,' she said brokenly. 'I can't imagine what it's like...' She bit her lip, fearing she was making things worse. 'You're having to re-live a tragedy. I'm so sorry.'

'It's not your fault,' he said curtly.

'Nevertheless, I feel responsible,' she ploughed on. 'You're being kind to me by hanging around but...' her voice shook '...I think you should leave and let me give a press conference or something. It would take the heat off you—'

Slowly he turned, unwillingly touched by her concern and courage. And she'd softened his anger. Taking her face between his hands, he gazed down at her.

'You're blameless,' he said quietly, disturbed by the brightness of her wide, silvery eyes. And her lashes were wet, as if she cared... He felt emotion welling up and clenched his jaw to quell it. 'You are totally innocent. And I'm afraid you have no idea what you're getting into,' he muttered under his breath.

She stood there, sweet and anxious, tiny pearly tears seeping from the corners of her eyes. Before he knew what he was doing, he'd kissed the latest droplets just before they reached her mouth. She shuddered. With pleasure.

He couldn't resist stealing a kiss from her softly parted lips.

And once he'd started there was no stopping him. He kissed her again and again, harder, deeper, searching passionately for her response and finding it. Her body was pressing against his, her hands mussing his hair as she pulled his head more surely down and a kick of excitement rocketed through him when he realised that she was as eager as he for this.

The softness of her mouth was extraordinary. The sweetness of it made him groan. She threw her head back and shook her glorious hair from its pins. He drew in a sharp breath of need and kissed her throat and the warm, delicate skin just behind her ear while she trembled in his arms and uttered satisfied little moans.

Slowly he eased her willing body towards the sofa, kiss by kiss, pushing her forward with his hips. She must know what he wanted. For the moment he was content to kiss her, to feel the soft, firm curves of her supple back and waist and hips beneath his palms.

'Sophia!' he whispered, sliding her skilfully onto soft cushions.

He saw the wonder in her eyes and tenderly kissed each delicate lid as he half lay across her. His mouth and fingers gently worked aside the straps of her dress. The feel of her silken, faintly perfumed skin against his lips was like an aphrodisiac.

Something else was happening to him; a choking surge of emotion was filling his heart and chest, making it difficult for him to breathe.

He didn't stop to question it. The needs of his body were driving him to take her chin between finger and thumb and kiss her senseless while he slid a shaky, questing hand to tentatively cup one full, high breast.

Sophia gasped but made no attempt to stop his exploration. Hazily she stared at him, utterly bewildered by what was happening. She couldn't believe that Rozzano found her attractive. Or that he wanted to kiss her, let alone... A warning sounded somewhere in the back of her brain. Why? it said. And she ignored it.

His smoky lids were lowered, the twin black curves of his lashes showing dark against his skin. As if in a dream, she saw his lashes lift till he gazed into her eyes. For a long time he held her gaze and she was incapable of looking away. Extraordinary things were happening to her. A melting of her flesh and bones. And there wasn't a scrap of sense in her brain. Only the fact that he was holding her and looking at her with sultry desire and she was being overwhelmed by an unstoppable joy.

Her arms came up and wound around his neck. Her lips curved into a slow smile and there was a glow of happiness in her eyes. Without knowing, she pressed against him, and found herself moving with a sensuality that was strange to her.

'*Bellissima Sophia,*' he muttered in a heart-lurching growl.

Fascinated, she watched his mouth shape into kissable, high arching curves. Her whole body trembled. He felt hard and muscular and utterly desirable. Parting her lips, she shaped her hands around his smooth neck and brought his head a fraction closer.

It was an invitation he didn't reject. His mouth descended on hers with a passion she welcomed. Her back arched automatically and he slipped the bodice of her dress down, his fingers brushing tantalisingly across the globes of her half-revealed breasts.

Then his mouth was there, drifting around each curve, slowly, slowly inching down the sprigged material until...

She went rigid. Her nipple was enclosed in moist warmth and it was being gently, agonisingly sweetly sucked, played with, and teased. She couldn't bear it. Fiercely she held his shoulders, digging her fingers in, her mind focussed only on that hard, taut centre from which came fiery darts of promise, shooting along nerve pathways to every part of her body.

Tousled and breathing heavily, he lifted his head and impatiently wrenched at his tie and top button.

'Help me!' he whispered hoarsely.

And, to her amazement, she did. Her palms touched his naked chest in awe, caressing the outline of his muscles while he brooded over her, his eyes black with passion. With a groan, she lifted her arms and put her hands

on his beautiful broad back, bringing him just close
enough for each engorged tip of her breasts to brush se-
ductively against his skin.

Why?

She tensed. She didn't know. And he must have de-
tected that something was amiss because he moved back
a little, watching her, his chest rising and falling with his
harsh breath, his lips parted, eyes pained...

Of course. A flash of anguish scythed through her.
He'd been distressed about his late wife. And she'd been
there, a pair of arms for him to fall into. A soft cushion
and a brandy would have done just as well, she thought
miserably.

His hand tentatively touched a coil of hair snaking over
her shoulders. 'Sophia?' he said gently.

She avoided his searching eyes. 'I'm sorry. I think we
ought to call a halt to this, don't you? They'll be coming
in to clean the room—'

'Not while there's a notice on the door. But if you
wish...' He eased himself away and stood, picking up his
shirt and slipping his arms into it.

Deeply embarrassed and shocked by her eager re-
sponses, she rearranged her dress and swung her long,
slender legs to the floor. They were trembling. And every
inch of her body was aroused and hungry. What a fool
she was, she thought bitterly. And wondered how on
earth she'd deal with the situation now.

'I'm the one who should apologise.' He slid his fingers
down her cheek and tipped up her chin. A faint frown
crossed his brow when he met her misty eyes. 'Forgive
me?' he asked huskily.

She swallowed. It was hardly his fault. 'Course!' she
managed, and pushed out a wavering smile, which he

kissed from corner to corner, very gently, a little lingeringly. And it took all her will-power not to kiss him back.

'I think you're right, we do need to get out,' he said
drily. 'Why don't you tidy your hair while I make a few
escape plans? Take your time. I'll need at least half an
hour.'

She nodded in relief and dashed for her bedroom, leaning back against the door with closed eyes and waiting
for her leaping heart to settle down. It refused. So she
scrubbed her hands in cold water and doused her face
then put on some lipstick and punished herself by yank-
ing her hair into a ballet-dancer's bun.

But she looked mutinous, her mouth pouting and full
as if demanding kisses. She drew in a long, shuddering
breath. She was hopelessly, deeply in lust and she wanted
Rozzano with every fibre of her being. But common
sense told her that he'd never touch her again.

So she made herself a cup of tea.

When she'd stalked up and down and read herself the
riot act for a while, she became aware of voices in her
sitting room. The escape committee? she wondered. And,
glad of anything to distract her simmering passions, she
took a deep breath and marched back into the sitting
room.

'Ah, there you are!' Rozzano gently took her arm and
drew her forward while she continued to gape.

Huge displays of flowers filled the room and several
men and women were fiddling with them in a rather pre-
tentious way. 'Gypsophila is *so* passé,' a florist was
drawling.

Sophia blinked at the discarded sprays of tiny white
flowers, which she knew as baby's breath. She didn't
know that flowers could be in or out of fashion. Stepping
back, her feet came into contact with a stack of boxes.

'Hats,' explained Rozzano.

'Hats.'

'And shoes and underwear.' He grinned. 'Grab the clothes you think will fit you,' he urged. 'You might as well make use of some of this stuff, even if they are a smokescreen.'

'But—!'

He beckoned to two women with armfuls of shoe-boxes. 'Trust me,' he ordered.

All became clear when they were sneaking through the hotel an hour later. She wore the manicurist's overall on top of her dress and a baseball cap low on her forehead. Sprays of eucalyptus filled her arms, almost obliterating her view. Somewhere behind her was Rozzano, his distinctive face hidden by the stack of hatboxes he carried.

Stifling their laughter, she and Rozzano clambered into the back of the florist's van and sprawled amongst squashed petals and crushed flower stems as it drove off through the traffic. After a decent interval, Rozzano shouted for the driver to pull over and let them out.

'How about that?' he asked smugly, lifting her down.

Grinning, she pulled off the cap and overall and pushed them into the back of the van. He thumped on the doors and the driver honked his horn then moved off.

'Brilliant!' she said breathlessly, pretending not to notice that he'd kept his hands on her waist. He was a 'toucher', she told herself. It was what he did with women. 'You're a brilliant organiser,' she said in awe.

'Years of practice. Venetians have a reputation for being quick-witted. You don't build a reputation as a nation of merchant princes without a certain amount of deviousness.' Rozzano lifted one hand and fiddled with her hair. 'Gypsophila. Stand still,' he ordered, when she fidgeted. His eyes twinkled into hers. 'Must get rid of it. Too,

too passé!' he drawled, his smiling face wonderfully close.

Sophia laughed. 'OK,' she said, coming back to practicalities, 'we escaped. But how do we get back?'

'No idea. I'll come up with something. In the meantime, after we've organised your passport, why don't we see the sights?' he suggested, tucking her arm in his. 'Tony told me there's a sightseeing bus that takes you to places like the Tower of London and the Houses of Parliament. You can get off wherever you like, and catch a later bus to continue the journey—'

'You, on a bus?' This she had to see!

'I have to admit it'll be a first,' he acknowledged, his mouth curving into a self-deprecating smile. 'I'm rather looking forward to it.'

That evening, in a tiny bistro somewhere in Mayfair, she slipped off her shoes beneath the minute, pleasingly intimate table and decided that this had been one of the happiest days of her life.

'My feet will never be the same again!' she groaned, wriggling her toes in relief.

Rozzano smiled and raised his glass to her. 'I'm not surprised. We must have walked miles.' His fingers caressed her cheek with heart-stopping tenderness. 'I've never had so much fun, laughed so much or been quite so anonymous. It was wonderful.'

'And your favourite part of the day?' she asked softly.

He hesitated, fingering the prongs of his pudding fork. 'The river trip. Without question.'

Her eyes went dreamy. He'd cuddled her, saying she must be cold. And once he'd kissed her exuberantly on the cheek and given her a squeeze, saying happily that he was having the time of his life.

With a kiss of her fingers, he excused himself from the table. Sophia sat in a contented daze, nibbling the mints that had accompanied the coffee. A while later, she watched him saunter back through the bistro, seeing how everyone stared enviously. She let the glow of happiness steal over her.

'Are you ready to go?' he murmured.

She arched an eyebrow. 'Depends. If I have to climb up the hotel rubbish chute, I need notice, a rope and a crampon or two.'

He leant forward and kissed her on the mouth, his eyes laughing at her look of astonished delight. 'Nothing so alarming. I've just organised a hide-away—a furnished flat for us to rent nearby. Let's check it out and make ourselves comfortable for the night.'

Her jaw dropped. 'But...our things are at the hotel!' she protested.

'They're being packed right this minute. A porter will bring them over,' he said airily, guiding her out and drawing her close for warmth in the still, cool night. 'This way. It's not far. Better than a hotel surrounded by the press, don't you think?'

'But it's nearly midnight! No flat agency can possibly be open—'

'The hotel manager pulled strings for me. Here we are.'

He had stopped outside a wonderful Georgian building overlooking a small square. Dazed, she followed him up the broad stone steps and waited while he rang a bell. A deferential young woman, about her own age but beautifully dressed and coiffed, opened the door and showed them around the enormous, ground-floor apartment.

It must cost an arm and a leg! Sophia thought. No. Two arms, two legs and an entire torso.

'I put some basic foods in the fridge as you suggested,' the woman purred, standing far too close to Rozzano.

Hating the woman's blatant invitation, Sophia pretended indifference by wandering into the huge stainless-steel kitchen to check out the giant larder fridge. Oh, yes. The usual stuff. Basic groceries. Champagne, caviare, quail and raspberries!

'Will it do?' Rozzano asked, appearing at the door.

She eyed him in mock exasperation. 'Not my brand of caviare, but—'

'Will it do?' he repeated, his stern frown ruined by the laughter tugging at the corners of his mouth.

'We have to sleep somewhere. It's too late to try anywhere else,' she said grudgingly.

Rozzano exhaled as if in relief, then came forward and kissed her softly on the mouth. The doorbell rang, making her jump, and they drew apart.

'Your luggage has arrived,' the agency woman announced. 'And would you sign the documents?'

'Shan't be a moment,' he promised Sophia. He pressed her hand. 'We'll be alone soon.'

What had he meant by that? As he went back into the drawing room, he turned and gave her a sultry, meaningful look which totally unnerved her. He couldn't be thinking of... No! It was impossible!

Sophia took several deep breaths. She could make a pot of tea, unpack, or let her bones melt into the floor. Close to surrendering to the latter, she supervised the moving of her case into one of the large double bedrooms. The maid who'd brought the luggage insisted on unpacking for her.

Sophia was startled to see that the designer outfits, shoes and gorgeous underwear had been mistakenly included. She'd have to speak to Rozzano about that, she thought uncomfortably.

The maid left. Feeling edgy about Rozzano's intentions, Sophia returned to the drawing room and slid back the heavy brocade curtains to stare out at the little park across the street. Typical of London's Georgian squares, it looked mysterious and magical in the light of the old street lanterns.

The outer door closed. She heard the sound of his footsteps coming slowly, relentlessly towards her and she went rigid, the hairs on the back of her neck standing up.

Had he set her up to continue what they'd started? She went cold, fearing he expected them to finish the day with a bedtime romp. But, as much as she secretly desired him, her principles were too ingrained for casual sex.

She'd tell him she was tired. Do a yawn or two. Say she felt sick, had mumps, cholera—anything to keep him at bay.

But... Her brow furrowed. Why had he been so attentive? She was far too ordinary. In the course of the day they'd passed a hundred women who were sexier, better groomed, more beautiful.

She froze, her eyes darkening with dismay. There could be another reason. During the river trip, he'd told her that some rich people became easily bored and jaded. They searched, he'd said, carefully watching her, for something or someone to amuse them.

A shiver ran down her spine. She'd thought he'd been warning her—but... Maybe he was preparing her and letting her know that she wasn't important to him, just fun, just different and an entertaining little episode in his life.

He paused right behind her and her breathing stopped altogether with fear. Disappointment flooded through her whole body. Her respect for Rozzano plunged. A wonderful day would be spoiled, a friendship would hit the dust. And she realised how much she'd been relying on him to help her through the next week or so. A sob rose to her throat but she masked it with a cough.

His hand pushed away her hair. She felt the pressure of his mouth on her bare neck and for a moment she let it stay there, her eyes closing in pained delight. Then she moved a fraction—but her action brought Rozzano's lips to her ear, which he nibbled so delicately that her whole body went into pleasurable paralysis.

'I lied to you when I said I enjoyed the river trip the most today,' he whispered.

Focussed on the sensations flashing through her and the bewildering immobility of her limbs, she dragged in a ragged breath to protest at his familiarity. 'Rozzano—!'

'Best of all,' he growled, slowly turning her helpless body around, 'was just being with you. Touching you. Holding you.' The darkness of his eyes blazed briefly with a fierce light and then became a fathomless black again. 'If I'm not careful, Sophia,' he muttered, 'I'll be falling in love with you.'

His mouth covered hers as it opened in blank astonishment and it was warm and moist, more voluptuous and arousing than anything she'd ever known. The kiss went on for ever and she knew to her consternation that she was utterly, fatally attracted to him and she wanted him to fall in love more than anything in the world. And yet she knew that almost certainly she would regret her infatuation—and any surrender she might make.

'Goodnight, Sophia,' he whispered, his breath sweet and tantalising on her lips. And before she'd jerked herself out of her stunned stupor he had gone.

* * *

During the next few days he overcame her doubts every time he touched her. She knew how stupid that was, but she couldn't stop herself from responding.

Together for every wonderful second from breakfast to bedtime, they behaved as lovers, laughing, chatting, or sharing long and happy silences and content to be in one another's company. But at night they went to their separate beds after long and searching embraces which left her feeling empty and frustrated, furious and desperately cheated.

As they walked back to the flat one afternoon, after exploring Dickens' London, she fell silent, knowing that she was falling in love. Yet in her heart of hearts she knew that he wasn't really serious about their relationship. It could only be an amusing fling, one he'd describe to his friends. There was no mileage in it and she'd get hurt.

Then they rounded a corner and came face to face with a crowd of assorted photographers and journalists.

'They've found us!' she wailed.

Rozzano's arms came protectively around her as he tried to push a way through. Cameras flashed and they were bumped and barged as photographers crouched to get a shot of their faces and reporters thrust microphones at them.

'Oy! Give us a break!'

'Sophia! Over here! Sophia!'

'You two shacking up together?'

She felt defiled, suffocated, and absolutely terrified. They were completely surrounded by jostling bodies. Gasping with fear, she looked around and saw staring, avid eyes and open, yelling mouths. Strangers shouted her name. Hands grabbed at her. She felt an elbow in her ribs, heard herself grunt with pain and then came

Rozzano's furious roar as he surged through them all, his sudden charge driving the two of them relentlessly to the door and the safety beyond.

At last she heard the door slam and collapsed in relief. Whimpering with frustrated anger at her feebleness, she let Rozzano carry her to her bed and revive her with a stiff brandy. He drew up a chair and sat close to her while her huge eyes stared at him in mute despair.

She lay there shuddering. 'It was like a pack of dogs hunting down deer,' she said in horror. 'And for what end? A page or two of gossip!'

The pack was still outside, making an awful racket. Fearfully she looked towards the curtained window, wishing she could drive them all away.

His fingers traced the faint bruises which were beginning to show on her skin, where she'd been pulled this way and that. 'I'm sorry.' Gently he kissed the scratch on her arm, made by someone's metal watch-strap.

She drew in a shaky little breath. 'Not your fault. It was awful. I don't want to go through that ever again!'

'I know,' he soothed, stroking her cold, clammy forehead. 'We can't go on like this, Sophia,' he said sternly. 'It has to end.'

End! She drew in a long, harsh breath of anguish. She wanted to catch him to her, to demand that he never left, but she managed to stop herself.

Her stomach muscles clenched convulsively. This was it. 'Yes,' she said dully.

'Good. I'll arrange for us to go to Venice tomorrow,' he said in a soft undertone.

Startled, she lowered her gaze. He wanted it to continue, then, to enjoy the novelty of seeing his city through her eyes. No. She wouldn't let him encourage her to amuse him and then dump her when she ceased to entertain him with her quaint country ways!

With great dignity, she sat up. 'You go. I've decided...' It had started well, but the words had stuck in her throat. Breathing quickly, her face as white as chalk, she forced herself to say what she must, speaking in a toneless babble. 'I think we should go our separate ways.'

'*What?*' he exclaimed in amazement.

She hurried on. 'There's no reason for me to stay in London now the press know where we are.'

He stared, his face paling visibly. 'No!' he objected beneath his breath.

'It's the most sensible solution. I'm going home. I'll get to Venice in my own time—'

He stood up sharply, his chair crashing over. She stared at him in surprise because he looked...shattered. Her heart stopped and then fluttered erratically.

'You can't go!' he muttered thickly. Then he shook his head, as if clearing it—and as if he too was astonished by what he'd said. She stared at him in shock, unable to comprehend the devastation in his eyes.

'What do you mean?' she asked faintly.

'It's perfectly simple! I mean I don't want to be parted from you!'

His impassioned voice had shaken with emotion. It was as if she'd delivered a bombshell and he was reeling from its blast. For the first time, she began to believe that he cared for her and she felt a surge of hope fill her with a dangerous joy.

He sat down on the bed and pulled her to him, a wonderful, urgent determination in every line of his face. 'I want you!' he muttered forcefully. 'No. Don't say anything. We don't need words. To hell with them!'

He was going to kiss her. Crushing her alarming joy,

she held him at bay, her hands pressing hard against his chest.

'We hardly know one another. You *can't* feel that strongly—!'

'I know I can't! It's madness. But I *do*!' he growled.

Her protest was muffled by the fierce pressure of his mouth. She felt herself being driven back, the softness of the bed meeting her spine while the hardness of his body and the feverish whispering in her ear made her resistance disintegrate into a million pieces. There was nothing she could do to stop him; all her will-power had gone beneath the onslaught of his desperate passion, the raw need in his eyes, his body, his searching, oh, so cruelly tormenting hands!

Seconds passed, or minutes—she didn't know. His need was so desperate that it totally overwhelmed her. They were locked together, their hands frantically clutching, mouths devouring.

He murmured that he wouldn't ever hurt her because he cared for her. Respected her values, admired her principles. He thought she was beautiful, funny, adorable, wise, clever, intelligent... The words flowed into her in a hot, passionate stream, destroying all her defences.

Because she felt the same about him.

How could she resist such an assault on her senses? His heart raced and pounded against her breast as they clung to one another convulsively. She had been close to losing him and her only instinct was to kiss him breathless, to grip his shoulders with all her strength as if in some way that might release the pent-up misery she'd been harbouring.

'I want to touch you, feel you, breathe you in through every pore...'

Mindless now, awash with pure happiness, she made

no murmur when he slowly—oh, too slowly!—slid away
her clothes. When he touched her, letting his fingers drift
tentatively down the curves of her body, his expression
of sweet anguish reached into her with a shattering force.

She was naked now, his lips setting her flesh on fire,
the depth of his desire so heart-wrenchingly intoxicating
that she wantonly encouraged him. Slowly he let his fingers trail to her thighs. And then he bent his head.

Sophia gave a hoarse cry, her body bucking in shocked
pleasure. 'Rozzano, no!' she croaked in panic.

His deeply intimate kiss filled her entire consciousness.
She groaned, wanting the soft melting inside her to go
on and on, hungry for its vibrating warmth as it spread
through her body. She was gasping, dizzy with hunger,
unable to stop herself from writhing on the tangled sheets
in hot desire. Whimpers escaped from her panting mouth,
her fingers tightening feverishly in his silky hair and sliding down to dig into his powerful shoulders.

It was an exquisite sweet pain that he was inflicting
and he too seemed to feel it, his body trembling on hers.
As her nerves strained to breaking point, he raised his
head. Every inch of her shook at the burning force of his
passion, the savage desire that had to be sated. She could
hardly breathe.

And then his lips enclosed her again, his tongue gently,
delicately creating havoc in the whole of her heart and
soul and mind till she didn't care about anything, only
the release of her long-suppressed need. Crying his name,
begging him not to stop, she clung to him, delighting in
his lovemaking, adoring him, wanting him to love her.

Except…he hadn't said those words she longed to
hear.

There had been no commitment. Of course there
hadn't. And so sex was out of the question.

With a despairing groan, she pushed him away, even though her body screamed at her for doing so.

'Wait! *No!*' she wailed, trying to sit up.

His arm hooked her back to him. 'Please, Sophia!' he said thickly. 'You can't—'

'I can!' she cried wildly, fighting him, beating at his chest. 'Please, Rozzano! I—'

Tears welled up in her eyes. How could she tell him that she wouldn't let any man be truly intimate with her unless he was her husband? You didn't mention the 'H' word a few days after meeting a man, she thought hysterically.

'Santa Maria!' he muttered, holding her fast. 'Don't you understand? I want you—'

'And I want you too! But that's not enough for me!' she sobbed. 'Let me go! I'm sorry I didn't stop you before but—'

'You didn't let me finish!' he muttered thickly.

Rozzano's grip eased and he slid her neatly alongside his body, still keeping her within the circle of his strong arms. He was panting, his breath hot and rasping on her naked shoulder. Sophia quivered from the sensation and bit her lip. It was her fault. She should have called a halt much earlier. But she'd wanted him so much.

'You mustn't finish,' she mumbled desperately.

'I meant,' he said drily, 'you didn't let me finish what I had to say—'

'You can't persuade me!' Squirming in embarrassment, she summoned up the courage to say, 'I—I don't believe in full sex outside marriage, Rozzano.'

His thumb gently but firmly tipped up her chin. 'But I never intended to go that far,' he told her gravely. 'For a moment I forgot who you were, what I was doing— everything. I don't know where I was. Paradise, I think.

Forgive me. I've never...' He scowled, perplexed. 'I lost control.'

'Explain to me where I stand with you. I'm not used to flirting and—and intimacy,' she told him, her cheeks flushed to a dark rose. 'You may think it's normal to seduce a woman after a few dinners but—'

'No,' he said quietly. 'I don't. That's not my way. You're the first woman...' He lowered his eyes and it was a moment or two before he had composed himself again and could look at her. 'I'm bewildered by what has happened to me,' he said. 'We've only known one another for a short time, although we've been together for almost every hour of the day. It's been an unbelievably intense experience for me—'

'And me,' she admitted in a small voice, summoning up the courage to stick to her decision, whatever excuse he came up with.

He smiled at her wary, tear-stained face and touched her pouting mouth with an affectionate finger. 'You've made one hell of an impact on me. I've never met anyone like you—never knew someone could be so perfect, so special.'

Sophia maintained the rigidity of her body. Words, she thought in distress. That was all they were.

'Over the past few days you've brought me to life,' he went on softly, caressing her face with wondering fingers. 'Until I met you, I was wrapped up in my grief. At first you made me laugh, made me feel relaxed and happy. Then...'

He swallowed. His tongue slipped around his lips and Sophia gazed at him, unable to breathe for tension. 'Then?'

'Then I knew something special was happening between us,' he said with restrained passion. 'These past few days have been wonderful. I never, ever want them to end.'

She closed her eyes in pain, her teeth biting into her lower lip as she struggled against the urge to surrender. It was sex, not love that he wanted.

He covered her throat in small, hot kisses, each one like a wound to her heart. 'Come to Venice with me tomorrow,' he coaxed. 'As my bride-to-be. I want you to be my wife, Sophia. Will you marry me?'

She was utterly speechless. It was the last thing she'd expected. If her life had depended on it, she couldn't have said a word.

'Answer me!' he urged. 'Don't keep me in suspense! I need to know *now*. Or,' he added, his eyes dark with determination, 'I'll make such mind-destroying love to you that you won't know what you're saying, and I'll damn well force you to say yes!'

'I— Why...?'

'Why do you think?' he asked passionately, tightening his hold on her shoulders. 'Sophia,' he husked, 'I'm crazy about you. I wake every morning with a smile on my face because I know we're going to be together. You know how good it's been for both of us. You must have realised how I felt! I look at you all the time, I am compelled to touch you—'

'I thought that was how you behaved with all women,' she said faintly.

'No.' He kissed her with a heart-stopping tenderness. 'I want to be with you all the time. To know that every day you'll be there. I want us to share our lives. I've thought about this, Sophia. It's not the decision of the moment. My dream is of us marrying, having children and growing old together.'

She felt herself sinking more deeply into his arms. 'Children!' she breathed, her resolve fatally weakening.

Babies of her own. Rozzano's babies. And she had believed she would never hold her own child in her arms, never be a mother! She pushed a shaking hand through her hair, her eyes wet with tears.

In her imagination she saw herself cradling a tiny, dark-haired baby, with Rozzano looking down on them both in wonder. They were in his *palazzo*, and the sound of a gondolier's love song came drifting in through the window—

'Sophia!' Rozzano's harsh, authoritarian voice brutally shattered her precious images as he gave her a little shake. 'You've got thirty seconds to answer. Yes or no?'

'I need time!' she wailed.

'You're not getting any.' His mouth hardened dangerously. 'How can you do this to me? Can't you see how I'm shaking? Decide with your heart, not your mind!'

Flustered, she tried to marshal her senses. In that eternity she weighed up the risks she was taking with her emotions. And, if she refused, the risk of regretting her decision for evermore.

There was no contest. She loved Rozzano and the thought of having his children made her want to weep with happiness.

Her eyes met his, locked, and blazed with an answering passion and love. She laid her head against his chest. Through the palm of her hand she could feel the frantic beating of his heart. Amazed that she could affect him so strongly, she lifted her face to his.

'Stay with me,' he whispered softly. His mouth grazed hers. 'Be my wife. Mother of my children...'

She lifted her heavy lids and saw that he was overcome by emotion. Deeply moved, she stroked his agonised face and smiled tenderly. 'Yes,' she said softly. 'Yes.'

CHAPTER FIVE

ON THE plane to Venice, she wore one of her new couture dresses; simple, understated and incredibly flattering. And on her left hand she *would* have worn an enormous diamond, the same misty blue as her dress, set in a terrifyingly valuable platinum ring.

Rozzano, however, had suggested when they chose it that it would be wiser if she kept it in her bag in case there was any media attention. And she'd instantly seen the sense in that. But she kept sneaking little glances at it!

Limp, stunned and deliriously happy, she had allowed Rozzano to make all the arrangements for their trip. She knew it had been madness to accept his proposal, that he *had* been insane with desire, surely, when he'd asked her to marry him. But twelve hours later he still seemed besotted.

'Now,' he purred, dipping a strawberry in Buck's Fizz and feeding it to her. 'We've got three weeks to make all the arrangements before our wedding day. Let's start with bridesmaids—'

'Rozzano!' she cried in horror. 'We can't get married that soon! It's crazy! We don't know each other. No, please hear me out!' she insisted, when he opened his mouth to argue. 'Marriage is much too important to take lightly. Six months would be more sensible—'

'Sensible! Who wants to be sensible?'

His eyes glittered and then he lowered his lids. But she'd seen the flash of annoyance in his gaze, and the stubborn set to his mouth. He didn't like being crossed, she thought apprehensively.

'Marriage is for keeps, Rozzano. It would be awful if we made a mistake—'

'You'll be marrying a madman by that time,' he muttered. 'I'm flesh and blood, Sophia! You don't know how hard it is for me to hold back!'

'We...' She moistened her lips and stared out at the Alps below, following the peaks and valleys, the icy crags punching through occasional clouds, the soft green lowland shimmering in the sunlight. 'You're not the only one who's...aroused,' she said bravely, blushing as she spoke. But she wanted him to know that she loved him enough to trust him. 'We could...' Her eyes pleaded with him to understand. 'Help me out, Rozzano!' she begged. 'You know what I'm trying to say!'

'You mean...we can ease one another's desires?' he suggested delicately.

Nervously she nodded and he closed his eyes in anguish, drawing in a huge, raw breath.

'*Four* weeks, then!' he said forcefully. 'You can't possibly ask me to wait any longer! We want to be together, don't we?'

'We will be—'

'I mean as man and wife. In the fullest sense, Sophia. You know the strength of my feelings. You can't doubt them. And think of your grandfather!' he said persuasively. 'He would like to live to see his great-grandchild. For his sake, we mustn't delay!'

Sophia wavered. His argument was convincing. She longed for Rozzano with a frightening hunger. And she had to admit that it would be wonderful for Alberto D'Antiga to enjoy the arrival of his great-grandson. Her heart softened. This time next year she could be a mother.

'So let's make babies as soon as we can,' Rozzano murmured wickedly into her ear.

'Unfair!' she protested. But he turned her face and lovingly, lingeringly kissed her mouth.

His eyes bored into hers, making her senses swim. 'Four weeks.'

'Four weeks,' she agreed with a helpless sigh.

He gave a delighted grin. 'That's wonderful! We'll be perfect together, Sophia. I know we will. So,' he said, smiling fondly at her, 'we'd better start planning the wedding of the decade!' His voice softened to a loving murmur. 'Tell me your wildest dreams, my darling. I will make them come true. Every one.'

'All I need is a man who loves me and to bear his children,' she said simply. A spasm of pain tightened his lips and she touched his hand with understanding tenderness. 'What is it? Are you thinking of your baby who was never born?'

He leant his head back against the seat, his eyes closed tightly. 'I was thinking that I couldn't bear it if anything should spoil our happiness,' he replied in a harsh undertone so laden with darkness that she felt a tiny trickle of fear run the length of her body.

Nervously, Sophia blinked in the bright sunshine as they walked through the terminal doors in Venice and out onto a landing stage. A man in white ducks hailed them and ran forward, enthusiastically greeting Rozzano.

'This is Mario,' Rozzano explained, when the man stopped pumping his hand up and down as if he might strike oil any minute. 'He's in charge of the family launches.'

Launches! thought Sophia as Rozzano gestured to a

palatial and sleek-looking boat with furiously polished brassware.

'*Buon giorno, contessa*. I am very pleased to say hello.'

She smiled, hiding her shock at being addressed by her title. She doubted she'd ever get used to it. 'I'm pleased to say hello, too!' she replied, genuinely delighted that they would be arriving by water.

But she was nervous, too, at the prospect of meeting her grandfather. Her hand shook in Rozzano's as he handed her into the boat though he made no sign that he'd noticed. She perched nervously on the immaculate royal-blue cushions, expecting him to sit beside her and hold her close to reassure her. But he didn't.

She tried not to mind but it did appal her that she should keep looking to him as if he were some kind of crutch. That wasn't the kind of relationship she wanted at all. But…did he?

The boat's engines roared into life, or she felt sure he would have heard the loud thudding of her heart. She wondered if he liked her vulnerability because it gave him a chance to be dominant. But she wasn't normally the vulnerable type. And when he found out he might drop her like a hot brick.

Butterflies swooped in her stomach and she folded her arms tightly over it as panic rose in her throat, threatening a cry of fear.

Perhaps their relationship was based on their own fantasies—a fairy tale of their own making…

Rozzano leant across to speak to her and with a supreme effort she produced a bright, interested face for him. 'We'll cross the lagoon,' he said, 'and you'll have a fantastic view of Venice, rising from the water.'

She nodded and concealed her quivering lip by swivelling around and watching the wake of the boat as it cut through the glassy water and changed the calm serenity of the surface into a froth of white foam. Rozzano tapped on her arm and reluctantly she turned back, wishing her emotions were flat and calm again.

'Look. See the *bricoli*—those huge poles in the water? They mark out the deep-water passages through the lagoon to the sea. And there's Torcello, the island where your ancestors and mine first settled.'

Sophia nodded, smiled and remained silent, her mind full of anxieties and worries. It had been a mistake to commit herself so hastily. She knew that now. They couldn't yet be certain of one another's love.

Her brows pulled together. Rozzano had spoken of his feelings with great eloquence. But had he mentioned love? She couldn't remember—her thoughts had been in such turmoil that half of what he'd said hadn't registered. Perhaps he had said he loved her. He'd been very sincere, very impassioned. Why would he propose if he didn't feel strongly?

Despite all her reasoning, she couldn't shake off her uncertainties. Only dimly was she aware of the beauty of the shimmering lagoon, and the tiny islands with roses and honeysuckle drifting over ancient brick walls.

And soon she could see the island of Venice itself sitting in the limpid water, the skyline a higgledy-piggledy mass of turrets and bell towers and domes and tiled roofs.

'They call Venice *La Serenissima*,' he said softly. 'The Most Serene.'

Tears of unexpected emotion collected in her eyes. Intending to share her feelings with Rozzano, she turned to him. He was staring at the city he loved and had eyes for no one and nothing else. She could see that he was utterly content. He'd come home.

The tug of destiny affected her, too. For the first time she began to comprehend fully what it meant to belong to a family which had occupied a piece of land for centuries. Preserving that family line would be almost a duty. No wonder her mother's actions had devastated the D'Antigas.

And now she was a part of that ancient dynasty herself—and would be helping to preserve it. Shaking off her nerves, she clutched her hands tightly in her lap and leaned forwards, studying everything intently, eager to learn something of her roots.

'Tell me what I'm seeing,' she said with quiet intent.

'We're coming up to the Basin of St Mark,' he obliged quietly. 'There…you see that bridge? And the one behind it, high above that narrow canal? The first is the Bridge of Straw and the other The Bridge of Sighs—'

'I remember. That's the bridge between the Doge's Palace and the prison.'

'It's completely enclosed so that convicted prisoners couldn't leap over the parapet and escape,' Rozzano explained, and gave a wry smile. 'However, the windows afforded them one last, tantalising glimpse of the city, the outside world—and freedom. Hence its name.'

'Cruel,' she commented.

His eyes flickered and grew distant. 'A streak of that cruelty still runs in some of us.'

Bitterness ran through his words. Startled, Sophia cast a quick glance at his face. There was a hardness there, a savage brutality to the line of his mouth. Yes, she thought, filled with chilling misgivings, she felt sure that he could explode into a violent fury if provoked. She swallowed, feeling suddenly apprehensive and horribly unsure of him.

Rozzano asked the boatman to stop for a moment and they bobbed up and down gently while she stared blankly, only managing with difficulty to focus on the beautiful pink marble façade of the Doge's Palace, with its graceful pillars and arcades.

'Just like the pictures,' she commented as brightly as she could.

Her heart raced alarmingly as she tried to quell her fears. He loved her. He wouldn't harm her. But the tension wouldn't leave her shoulders and she sat rigidly, like a terror-stricken child, desperate to overcome her irrational sense of dread.

He rested his arm on the back of the cushion, his expression gentling. 'They say that if a sixteenth-century Doge were to appear now he'd find Venice much the same,' he told her with husky affection. 'Now—see the bell tower, the Campanile? And as we move on you'll catch a glimpse of the domes of the Basilica of St Mark. It's beautiful, Sophia. Wildly over-the-top, and stuffed with ancient treasures. I'm really looking forward to showing it to you.'

Nothing was wrong, she told herself. She was being fanciful. Conscious of the long silence, she attempted to curb her over-active imagination and make some kind of intelligent comment.

'Father said the whole city is built on tiny islands and mud flats. Those buildings are massive, though. Was he right? It doesn't seem a very reliable foundation.'

And her marriage, a little voice nagged. How safe were the foundations for that?

'Reliable enough to last for several centuries,' he said, amused. 'Millions and millions of stakes and solid plat-

forms underpin the buildings. You look apprehensive.'
He laughed. 'Don't worry! The D'Antiga *palazzo* won't
collapse—I've seen to that. I've spent a good deal of time
restoring it.'

He'd been genuinely good to her grandfather, she
thought. Looking after the D'Antiga affairs must have
made heavy demands on Rozzano.

'I'm relieved. I'd hate to see the whole city sink before
I've had a chance to explore it,' she said drily.

He grinned. 'No chance! Even though people take a
lifetime discovering its treasures.' His eyes danced as he
leaned closer and murmured, 'That's my intention with
you.'

Her heart leapt with joy. Happily she flung away her
worries and basked in his smile. 'Be*have*! And get on
with the commentary or I'll hitch a lift on a tour boat.'

'You English have no soul!' he reproached with a the-
atrical sigh. 'OK, I surrender. Commentary. Stating the
obvious, we're coming to the Canalazzo—the Grand
Canal. Look and be amazed.'

She did, and she was. Nothing had prepared her for
the images which were unfolding before her eyes. As
they entered the broad canal, they became part of the
pageant of sleek launches and gondolas, little ferries and
huge barges which bustled up and down the waterway.
And on either side soared the palaces, each one different
and forming a magical backdrop to the busy scene.

'That's Ca' Barbarigo—seventeenth-century, Ca'
Dario—with a fifteenth-century façade on an older,
Gothic building, Ca' Grande—sixteenth-century…that
one there's twelfth, that's thirteenth-century…'

Her head was spinning as he named them in loving
tones, almost as if they all belonged to him personally.
And she began to realise for the first time the enormity

of what she was taking on and how much she would need Rozzano's good advice.

'I could look on this scene for the rest of my life and never tire of it,' she said softly.

'I think that could be arranged!' he teased. 'And... ah...what about this *palazzo*? Interesting, do you think?'

She followed his pointing finger and sighed in pleasure. 'For once you've made an understatement. It's fabulous.'

It rose majestically, five storeys high from the canal, boasting a dozen blue and white striped *bricoli* and several small landing stages sheltered by royal-blue awnings. Above a vast arched door that met in a graceful point were delicate stone balconies with pillars surrounding tall arched windows, each of which was intricately latticed.

'Glad you think so.' Rozzano's voice had shaken a little. She turned enquiringly, but his eyes were fixed keenly ahead on the honey-coloured building as the launch turned towards it. And his smile was beatific as he said, 'This has been my home for the past five years.'

Her eyebrows lifted in surprise. 'Now I understand your eagerness to come home to your *palazzo*!' she said enviously.

He gave an enigmatic smile and, to her surprise, he motioned the boatman to tie up to the jetty.

'Is this where we get off?' she asked. 'Are we to walk to the D'Antiga palace?'

She felt a slight disappointment. It would have been lovely if her grandfather's house had been on the Grand Canal itself, but it seemed it must be in the maze of back alleys and canals beyond.

'Only the Doge's palace is called a *palazzo*. All the other palaces are called "houses". And this particular

one,' he said softly, as he handed her onto the landing
stage, 'is the Ca' D'Antiga.'

Astonished, she whirled, alerted by the love in his
voice and the passion lurking in his eyes. A fool could
have deduced that he felt deeply about this breathtaking
palace.

And yet it didn't belong to him. Her grandfather owned
it...and one day it would be hers. She shivered despite
the warmth of the sun. Something was nagging in the
back of her brain. A terrible, treacherous thought that she
wouldn't allow to surface.

'But...don't you have a home of your own?' she asked
jerkily. Bewildered, she noted the increased tension in
his hand where it gripped her elbow.

'Yes,' he said, sounding faintly strained. 'I own Ca'
Barsini. It's further up, near the Rialto Bridge.'

He paused for a moment at the sound of a siren. His
arm came around Sophia's waist as an ambulance boat
roared past, trailing a wail of sound and producing a
strong wake that rocked the pontoon.

'Why don't you live there?' she pursued, disappointed
that he hastily detached himself the moment the movement had stopped.

'Because my brother and his wife and children are
there. Enrico can entertain to his heart's content—he's a
very social animal,' he said with detectably false enthusiasm. Seeing her questioning eyes, he added reluctantly,
'Enrico needs to be out of my shadow. Elder brothers can
be hard to live up to. It's important he has his own life.
I've made this my home because your grandfather likes
to have me around. We're very close.'

'You've obviously been devoted to him,' she conceded
slowly.

But why? her mind kept demanding. And she was determined to find out. Fluttering nerves skittered up and down her body as he propelled her towards the watergate.

'Wait a minute!' she said suddenly. She fumbled in her bag and took out her ring, slipping it on her finger. 'The press won't leap on us indoors,' she said, happily turning her hand this way and that. It was beautiful. Rozzano's commitment to her. Now she felt properly engaged.

'Sophia...' He studied his shoes. Every ounce of his body was rigid with tension.

She stiffened in apprehension. 'What is it?' she asked uneasily.

'I don't know how to say this...'

His hard, uncompromising profile said it for him. Bad news was on the way. She steeled herself, shutting out the horrid little voice which said that her happiness had been too good to last.

'Go on!' she challenged quietly.

It seemed he couldn't speak for a moment and that made her even more jittery. Then, in a rush—as if eager to get his speech over with—he said, 'I think the sudden announcement of our engagement might be too much for your grandfather to take.'

Sophia felt her body freeze. All her doubts crystallised. He wanted to keep it a secret, she thought, and she realised that she'd *never* been totally sure of Rozzano, otherwise she wouldn't be leaping to such a terrible conclusion. She was so insecure in his love that it was even possible for her to wonder if this was his way of easing out of the relationship. A gentle let-down now, a gradual drifting away, and she'd be sidelined before she knew it...

But, part of her argued, he'd bought a valuable ring.

Why propose to her and then drop her within the course of a day or so? He'd gained nothing. Yet.

Her head ached. Why was she thinking these shocking things about Rozzano? She loved him! She should trust him implicitly!

'Speak to me, Sophia,' he said harshly.

Stone-cold despite the warm air, she knew her voice would betray her hysteria and so she kept her response to a brief, 'What are you suggesting we do?'

Beside her she felt the hiss of exasperation as it was expelled through his teeth. 'Keep it a secret for the time being. I know what I'm asking, but you must see my point of view. He's emotionally fragile, Sophia. Your arrival will be all he can cope with. Please understand. I care about him very much. He's treated me like a son. Let's wait till we think he's ready.'

'A short time ago we were getting married in a rush because of him,' she reminded him sharply.

That brought a quick frown to his face. 'We *are*! But let's take one step at a time with him—'

'Are you ashamed of me?' she accused, her eyes as dark as charcoal.

'No!'

Clearly angry at that suggestion, he was nevertheless struggling for words to explain. Tell me you love me, her eyes pleaded. Reassure me.

He shot her a quick glance but never saw her plea— or, if he did, he ignored it. 'Give him a week, ten days at most to get over the excitement of meeting you,' he said shortly. 'It won't be easy for him, seeing you. I expect your appearance will bring back to him some painful memories of your mother.'

'I suppose so,' she conceded reluctantly.

'It needn't make any difference to us,' he coaxed. 'We

can go ahead and make all the arrangements then tell him gently.'

At least he was still talking about making preparations for the wedding, she consoled herself. She relaxed a little. 'Will he disapprove?' she asked bluntly.

'I think he'll be delighted. Give him breathing space first. I'd hate the excitement to become too much for him.'

How could she refuse? It would seem churlish. But she hated the idea, even though it made perfect sense. Her tapered fingertip smoothed over her beautiful ring. Stupidly, her lower lip wobbled.

Seeing she was close to tears, Rozzano hastily pushed open the heavy oak door and drew her into the privacy of a huge and airy entrance hall.

She stared numbly down its length to the slender colonnades of a sunny courtyard beyond. She barely registered the scent of honeysuckle drifting from the open windows, though normally she would have commented on it in delight.

But she was too panic-stricken about removing the symbol of their love. Maybe it was superstitious nonsense, but without it she felt that their relationship would definitely founder.

However, she wouldn't defy him. Her grandfather's health was too important. She realised that her relationship with Rozzano would live or die for more reasons than the fact she wore his ring.

'You're right,' she said, generously giving him the benefit of the doubt. 'I'll take it off.'

Gently she eased the ring up her finger though she was unable to stop her mouth from drooping with misery. It could have been a trinket they'd chosen from a cheap store and she would have been just as upset about re-moving it.

Feeling forlorn, she slipped it from her finger and re-turned it to the zip pocket of her bag. All the time she was wishing that he would kiss her, and persuade her that everything was all right.

'*Principe!*'

'Flavia!' All smiles suddenly, he hurried forward and, to her astonishment, embraced a grey-uniformed, middle-aged maid. There was a little joshing and plenty of laugh-ter and then she was introduced. 'Flavia has known me all my life,' he said, as the two women shook hands warmly. 'Her mother was Father's cook. Don't be sur-prised if you find her giving you advice. Our families are so intertwined that she has an opinion on everything we do—and sometimes she treats me like a brainless brother!'

Sophia gave a weak smile. He spoke again to Flavia and then she left them.

'Come upstairs to the salon,' he said lightly. 'We'll wait there. I've asked Flavia to tell your grandfather we've arrived.'

Very much at home in his surroundings, he led the way up the grand double staircase. Sophia swallowed nervously, intimidated by the massive oil paintings of haughty-looking men and women who must be her an-cestors.

This was all too much for her to handle! She hesitated, filled with an overwhelming urge to turn tail and run, but Rozzano pressed her hand, moving her on again, and she looked up at him gratefully, glad of his understanding.

But when he spoke she discovered why he was ca-ressing her. It wasn't out of sympathy at all.

'I know I shouldn't be touching you and that makes

the situation highly arousing.' He gave her a wicked glance with his smouldering eyes. 'We must pretend to be polite strangers when people are around. Hell! I'll go mad with frustration! I'll live for the night, when I can sneak to your room and we can make passionate love to one another.' His voice curled into every corner of her body, heating it, coaxing her with its sensual murmur. He lowered his pitch. 'Think of it, Sophia! It'll be fun.'

Fun. Her skin prickled in warning. It was a game to him! A game of 'don't touch', delicious and forbidden—like the games men played with their mistresses when their wives were around.

Fun. Her heart sank. He'd have sexual satisfaction without responsibility. And each day she'd have to pretend she didn't care for him at all. No. Her mouth firmed in mutiny.

'I can't—won't—live a lie,' she said flatly. 'I had no idea you meant me to pretend that I hardly know you.'

His eyes narrowed. 'I'm not asking you to lie, just to contain your feelings. We've both been forced into that strait-jacket before. You've been used to doing that all your life,' he threw back at her in a hoarse rasp, a horrible harshness roughening the normal musical rise and fall of his lyrical voice.

'And I don't want to do it again!' she cried passionately. 'I want to be what I am! To show emotion when I feel it, to laugh and sing and cry...'

Her voice faded away, her throat blocked with choking misery. She wanted to show her love for him, not to hide it as if it were something shameful.

But a single-minded determination glittered in the unreadable depths of his dark eyes. 'I understand that. I have my reasons for asking you to do this. Good reasons.

You mustn't show that you care for me. Promise me, Sophia!' he said in a fierce hiss.

She halted at the top of the stairs, shocked by his vehemence. Sweet heaven! she thought in horror. Everything was going wrong. Had she made a terrible mistake? Perhaps there really had been a hidden agenda for his whirlwind courtship, something even more sinister than the titillation of a tired palate!

She would have swayed, but pride steadied her. Until she knew what was really behind his proposal, she would resist any attempt by him to hurry her into marriage. If that was what he'd ever intended.

Her legs wobbled as if she were on shifting sands. But she only had herself to blame. She'd been too ready to believe him, too eager to fall for the rosy, romantic future he had painted. Not any more.

Angry and upset, she gritted her teeth and forced a smile even though she felt her heart would break.

'I'll show no sign of affection in public, you can be sure of that.'

'Excellent!'

Out came the dazzling grin, right on cue. It was as if clouds had momentarily obscured his face, she thought miserably. Now he was getting his own way—as he believed—the sun had come out again.

Her own smile wavered a little as they walked the length of a barrel-vaulted gallery. So Rozzano needed to be dominant. Sophia drew herself up proudly. No man would rule her. If he thought she would be a pushover, he was in for a nasty shock!

'Actually,' he said silkily, 'I think it might be a good idea to keep our wedding a secret from everyone but Alberto till the latest possible moment.'

'Oh? Why?' she asked shortly, her mouth set in a stubborn line.

'It's occurred to me that no one would be able to interfere. We can decide on ten bridesmaids or none and dress them in cream silk or Lycra with purple spots—'

'I think you have a bridesmaid fixation,' she said tartly. 'How do we get people to turn up?'

'Easy. We invite them to a grand celebration ball.' His eyes danced with amusement. 'Imagine, Sophia! They'll be astounded when you arrive in your wedding dress!'

'What fun,' she observed drily.

He chuckled, not recognising her sarcasm. 'No one will forget our wedding! And I've just realised—there'd be one great bonus. The press wouldn't get wind of it and we'd be able to stop our wedding day from becoming a fiasco.'

'You're very thoughtful.'

He gave her a suspicious glance but she'd found a serene expression from somewhere and he nodded in satisfaction. 'Agreed, then?' he murmured lightly.

Too lightly. Despite his casual manner, it was obvious that he desperately wanted her to fall in with his plans. And perhaps it did serve her purposes. If no one knew they were to be married, her shame would remain a secret if the wedding were cancelled.

'Why not?' she replied, attempting a carefree shrug.

But Sophia's stomach was churning with unnamed fears. If he was rushing her into marriage, if he wanted it to be concealed from everyone he knew...was there something she didn't know about, a reason for the haste and his desperate desire for secrecy?

Please, no! she begged the Fates. Don't let him deceive me! If he should prove to be false... She clutched at her breast, her eyes huge with distress. She'd die of misery, she thought dramatically—but she'd make sure she crippled him first!

'The salon.' Totally relaxed now, he opened a pair of double doors. 'Welcome,' he said, as if he were the host and she the guest.

Faintly annoyed by that, she entered the high-ceilinged room and gasped in awe.

'Lovely, isn't it?' he murmured with more than a hint of possessive pride. 'Make yourself at home. May I get you a drink?'

She looked to where he stood, decanter already in his hand. As if he owned the place, she thought, and then wiped that from her mind. 'No, thank you,' she said politely. 'I think it might give a bad impression if I breathe whisky all over my grandfather at our first meeting.'

'You're right!'

He was grinning, pouring himself a drink as if he didn't have a care in the world. Why should he have, when she'd obediently agreed to everything he'd suggested? She gritted her teeth, determined to hide her anger.

Desperate to do something, she walked to the tall windows. They ran from floor to ceiling and opened onto a small stone balcony above the Grand Canal, which glittered in the bright sunshine.

From where she stood she could see the dome of the Salute church and clusters of exotic black gondolas tied to barber-striped poles outside ochre-coloured palaces. It was an incredible setting, of breathtaking beauty.

Her hand had been resting against the heavy oyster-coloured drapes framing the window. Almost without thinking, she let her fingers trail over the sensual silk, her newly heightened senses revelling in their voluptuous opulence. Behind her, she heard the faint hiss of Rozzano's breath.

Her back stiffened. So he didn't like her touching D'Antiga possessions! After all, he'd spent years treating them as his own...

Like an arrow, the treacherous suspicion shot into her mind again, only to be fiercely dismissed. If she and Rozzano had any chance together, she had to stop inventing reasons for his behaviour—especially when she had no hard evidence.

Taut with nerves, she deliberately set about touching a few more items. A bronze statue. An intricately inlaid marble table. The gilded frame of a huge oil painting depicting Adam and Eve in swirling draperies and little else. And as she did so the pressure in the room seemed to hitch up a notch or two.

Her stomach swooped. He hated her being there! Touching what he regarded as *his* things!

'Carpaccio,' he said tersely, coming to where she was studying an oil painting. His tension was so palpable that it electrified the air.

Her heart fluttered frantically against her ribcage. 'I know nothing about painters. Is he famous?' she asked politely, wishing her grandfather would appear and rescue her from this vile atmosphere. And once, she thought wanly, she'd loved being alone with Rozzano!

'One of the masters. Do sit down,' he said politely.

Host to guest again! 'Thank you,' she answered coolly, heading for a comfortable armchair.

He began to sift through letters on a gilded antique table, opening one or two, stuffing the others into his pocket. And then he took up the classic male pose of ownership, standing in front of the marble fireplace, one elbow casually on the mantelpiece as he sipped his drink and looked at her inscrutably from under his lashes.

Sophia hid her mounting anxieties and crossed one elegant, Vianni-shod ankle over the other. 'I'm beginning to enjoy luxury. I feel really at home here,' she announced, injecting a proprietorial note into her voice to test him.

Rozzano's brows drew together in a hard black line and it gave her no pleasure that she'd apparently hit a raw nerve. 'Good. You certainly seem very composed,' he clipped out.

'It's the clothes,' she replied casually. 'They have confidence sewn into the seams. I probably look as good as I ever will.'

'Captivating,' he agreed, a faint curl to his mouth. 'I'm having difficulty keeping my hands off you.'

It wasn't noticeable, she thought tartly. And wanted to weep. Her eyes pricked with hot tears. She didn't want doubts or mysteries. Just Rozzano. She'd have it out with him, clear the air... Her spiky lashes lifted but he was listening to something inaudible to her, his head cocked on one side.

'Your grandfather's coming,' he said suddenly. 'I recognise that creaking floorboard!'

And he was across the room, opening the doors to a nurse who was pushing an elderly, white-haired man in a wheelchair.

'Rozzano!' Alberto D'Antiga held out his arms and the two men embraced fondly, murmuring to one another with affection.

Sophia watched, her emotions skittering this way and that. The love between them was plain to see and it gladdened her aching heart.

Despite her grandfather's frailty, it was obvious that

he had once been an imposing man. He was tall, and sat erect like a soldier on parade, and he reminded her so much of her beloved father that her eyes became misty.

'And you must be my Sophia!'

Smiling gently at the warmth in his tone, she went to him, knelt beside the chair and allowed herself to be wrapped in his thin arms. For a long time he held her, emotion shaking his gaunt frame. And she couldn't speak, couldn't say any of the words she'd planned, the little phrase of Italian she'd learnt to please him. Whatever his titles and noble ancestry, he was her only living relative and his affectionate welcome had won her heart already.

His hand lightly stroked her hair. 'Ah! So like your mother!'

Sophia pulled away a little, sitting back on her heels and blinking back the unshed tears. 'Flatterer!' she reproached, emboldened to tease him by the lively twinkle in his eyes. 'Mother was beautiful—'

'And so are you,' he assured her, touching her flushed and happy face.

'I think,' she said in amusement, 'that you're horribly biased.'

With an immaculate linen handkerchief, he dashed away the tears that had fallen to his cheeks and sighed. 'Forgive an old man's weeping, Sophia. Seeing you means so much to me. I believed that I was the last of the D'Antiga bloodline. It broke my heart that I had no descendants.'

'Would you both excuse me?' Rozzano fingered his trilling mobile phone.

'Of course! All of Venice must know you've returned!' Alberto said indulgently. His doting eyes followed

Rozzano as he strolled to the far end of the salon and answered the call.

'You love him very much,' Sophia ventured. It was as if, she thought ruefully, she wanted someone—anyone—to praise him, and thus to allay her fears.

'He has become my son,' D'Antiga said simply. He squeezed her hand. 'I was very lonely till he came here. And now he has brought you to me! So generous, so typical of him when he stands to lose everything because of you!'

Sophia froze. Her hands tightened convulsively in her lap. 'Gracious! How?' she jerked out.

'My dear, he married little Nicoletta, a distant relative of mine. She was the only remaining D'Antiga apart from me. And then she died.'

Sudden tears filled her eyes and she stared at her trembling fingers to hide them. Rozzano hadn't told her that Nicoletta had been a D'Antiga. Her mouth twisted. How economical with the truth he was!

'I knew he'd married and his wife had died in childbirth. I didn't know about the connection,' she said, hardly able to breathe.

'Nicoletta was my last hope,' grumbled her grandfather. 'It was an excellent union between our two families! And it brought me so much happiness when Nicoletta said she was pregnant.'

She struggled to comment. 'It was a tragedy that she died so young. It must have been a terrible shock for you all.'

Her grandfather's eyes were pained. 'Yes, but Rozzano felt the blow the hardest. He's always been so strong and capable, coping with emergencies, tragedies... He was very brave when his parents died in a boating accident out on the lagoon—and he was only eighteen. He took over the business as if he'd been doing it all his life and became a father and mother to Enrico. But when Nicoletta died he was inconsolable. He went to pieces and we didn't see him for days after the funeral. I've never known a man to look so deeply shocked. It was as if his world had come to an end.'

She felt very sad. This was confirmation that Nicoletta had been Rozzano's great love. How could she compete with that?

Stiffly she got to her feet, knowing the truth behind Rozzano's interest in her. 'So that's what you meant, Grandfather. Rozzano became your heir!' she said steadily, amazed that her bitterness could be kept so strictly in check. But she didn't want to hurt the old man. He'd be devastated to know what Rozzano had been planning.

'Of course. But now,' said her grandfather tenderly, catching her cold, lifeless hand, 'you will inherit the D'Antiga fortune instead. See how honourable he has been, not to discourage you?'

'The extent of his honour amazes me,' she fudged. Her heart was breaking. He'd really fooled her! How could he! How *dared* he?'

Alberto chuckled. 'Keep looking over your shoulder, Sophia!' he joked. 'We must make sure Rozzano doesn't push you into the lagoon!'

She laughed, though the sound rang false to her sensitive ears. 'He wouldn't do that,' she declared as brightly as she could.

Why would he, she thought angrily, when he could marry her instead and get a nursery full of children first, and secure his rights to the D'Antiga fortune? It was no wonder that he'd been agitated at the solicitor's, when he'd first learned that her mother had had a child!

And how clever, how quick-witted he'd been to see

that he had the answer to his problems right in front of him, in the guise of a simple country girl who'd be flattered and only too thrilled to be courted by such a handsome, passionate prince!

Damn him! she cursed, so consumed with anger that she could hardly breathe. Then she realised her grandfather was speaking, and for his sake she tried to pay attention and *not* to throw daggers of hatred at the lying, cheating deceiver silhouetted like a lounging Adonis against the tall window.

But when she turned back she kept the image of Rozzano in her grieving heart and it wouldn't go away, no matter how hard she tried to replace it.

'...wouldn't behave like that. You have judged him well. He is too kind, too generous,' the old man was saying softly. 'Trust him,' he urged Sophia. 'He is the finest man. You can rely on him to help you in the running of our business.' He shook his head in mock bewilderment. 'Once I could understand it all, now it's too complicated—and I'm allergic to computers!'

Unwilling to worry her grandfather, she stretched her face into a smile. 'Give me a bit of paper and a pen any day!' she agreed cheerfully.

Alberto sighed in sympathy. 'We'll leave it all to him, shall we?'

'Does he take a salary for the work he does?' she asked innocently.

Her grandfather chuckled. 'He doesn't need money! He's probably richer than I am! I'm afraid his family did rather well out of the Crusaders,' he confided. 'Charged them exorbitant prices for accommodation on their way to the Holy Land. No, Sophia. He runs the business because he is that kind of man—though I think he would like more time to check on his publishing empire.'

So he didn't need money. Unless he was greedy, and had empire-building plans. Her eyes gleamed. Vowing that *she* would take the reins, that Rozzano wouldn't run rings around her, she pressed his hand in excitement.

'We must give him more time to himself. I think I should know the ins and outs of D'Antiga's. I want to become familiar with every aspect of the business.' Her face was alive with enthusiasm. 'If there's anything I don't understand, Rozzano can explain over and over again until I've got it. I'll work hard, Grandfather, and you'll be proud of me!'

'Such fire! Such drive!' he admired wistfully. 'I admire you, Sophia. I have no fears about turning our fortune over to your care.'

'I'll start tomorrow,' she promised.

Her eyes flashed in Rozzano's direction but he was murmuring into the receiver as if talking to a lover, his body leaning comfortably against the cream panelled shutters, his free hand idly tracing the gold leaf cherub in the centre.

Something sharp and hot sliced into her body. Love and hate, ice and fire. Every movement he made was sensual, graceful even. The soft arc of his mouth caressed his words lovingly. His thick fringe of lashes fluttered appealingly on to-die-for cheekbones. His stance was re-laxed—but he gave the impression of suppressed energy and drive nevertheless. And he was smiling with satis-faction...rather like a panther after a kill.

Her body melted to the core. She wanted him. And hated him too.

'My ancestors began by trading spices from the Orient, you know,' her grandfather said, his eyes far away as he focussed on some distant memory. 'Then we changed to specialising in perfumes—'

'Mother had wonderful perfumes!' Sophia cried shakily.

'Did she?' D'Antiga's mouth quivered. 'Forgive me,' he said emotionally. 'Forgive me the wrong I did to her!'

She held his shaking hands in hers and on an impulse drew them to her warm cheek. 'Let's forget the past,' she said unsteadily. 'We'll talk about Mother another day, shall we?'

'Bless you, child, for your compassion. And now, if you'll excuse me, I am tired. We will have lunch tomorrow, yes? Press that bell if you will, for the nurse. Thank you. Oh…ask Rozzano to arrange for me to see a lawyer to change my will in your favour. I am impressed by what Rozzano has told me about you, dear child. A young woman who cares for her sick father for so many years must have very special qualities.' He kissed her affectionately. '*Ciao, Sophia.* You've made me happy again.'

Lovingly she embraced him. Rozzano hastily broke off his call and accompanied her grandfather to the door, his hand resting lightly on the old man's shoulder. And when they parted Sophia was unwillingly touched by the little bow that Rozzano gave, a bow of respect and affection.

But now she had the answer to all her niggling doubts, all the pieces of the jigsaw puzzle that wouldn't fit. Rozzano had pursued her because she embodied everything he wanted: the *palazzo*, the D'Antiga fortune, a gullible mind and, she thought grimly, child-bearing hips.

Perfect. What more could a mercenary Venetian prince want? The pain seemed to shrink her heart but she set her teeth against it. She wouldn't allow him to hurt her. He wasn't worth grieving over.

'I'm tired too,' she announced coolly when they were

alone again. 'I'll go to my room and unpack and perhaps wander around the house—'

'Of course. Let me know when you're ready,' he said quickly, 'and I'll escort you—'

'No, thanks. I want to take my time and explore on my own.'

'Sweetheart! You don't have to keep up the distant manner when we're in private,' he said softly.

Her blazing eyes challenged his. 'Will anger do instead?' she snapped.

'Sophia! What—?'

'Don't come near me!' she spat. 'You didn't tell me your late wife was a D'Antiga! You didn't say you were my grandfather's heir! Why, Rozzano? Did you have a secret agenda? Would you like to share it with me?'

He stared, struck speechless by her outburst.

'Lost for words?' she taunted. 'Surely not! You, the most glib-tongued man I've ever met? You must have been appalled when you discovered my mother had given birth to a child—'

'If you remember correctly,' he replied tautly, 'I was delighted.'

She frowned, confused. Yes. That was how it had seemed. Uncertainly she eyed him, trying to work out why, but he spoke before she could come up with an answer.

'You were the reason I didn't tell you I'd become the D'Antiga heir,' he snapped, his face stiff with contained anger. 'You were thinking of turning down your inheritance for several reasons of your own, weren't you?'

'Yes, but—'

'So why didn't I encourage your doubts?'

Her frown deepened. 'I don't know—'

'I could have worked on your fears but I didn't,' he

bit out. 'I kept quiet about my connection with your grandfather because I could see you had unusually high moral standards, and I felt that you might be uncomfortable at the thought of disinheriting me. I was anxious not to put any obstacle in your way. I wanted you to acknowledge your link to your grandfather, for *his* sake.'

She chewed this over for a moment. 'OK, what about later, when I was more sold on the idea?' she shot at him. 'You had a chance to tell me then!'

Sadness touched his eyes and mouth for a brief moment. And then his expression became a mask. 'We seemed to be busy with other things,' he said quietly. 'Falling in love, for instance.'

The wound pierced through her. In anguish, she hung her head. She couldn't stand the sight of him any longer. Part of her wanted to run to him, to find that scrap of love and warmth which he'd shown her and to wrap herself in it. Part of her wanted to pummel his chest and scream away her fury at being deceived.

'I'm going to my room,' she muttered. 'No! Don't show me! There are maids, aren't there?'

But his body barred the door. Suddenly he looked large and intimidating, the blackness of his eyes piercing her with their chilling anger.

'You're wrong about me,' he said tautly. His head went up and he looked down his patrician nose at her, silently demanding her capitulation and an abject apology.

'Maybe you're wrong about me!' she flung. 'That's the danger of not knowing anything about one another! I did warn you, Rozzano!'

Silver lights flashed across the dark eyes. 'Meaning?'

'Maybe I'm not as submissive as you think—'

'All the better. I want a wife who is my equal,' he replied exasperatingly, ruining her defiant stance.

'Do you?' she challenged. 'A woman who defies you? Wilfully disagrees with everything you wish? No, I thought not!' she declared, seeing the gradual tightening of his mouth. 'Don't imagine that because I'm a vicar's daughter I'll roll over like a doting dog and accept everything you do! I'm not a simple sweetie with a heart of gold. I have feelings. Opinions of my own—'

'I don't expect obedience. What a ridiculous idea!' he said quickly. 'But you have the sense to see when a course of action is wise—'

'Suddenly I'm tired of being wise. Sometimes I feel like going off the rails. Maybe I'll blow my inheritance!' she said wildly. 'All this could go to a girl's head!' she declared, waving a hand at the sumptuous room.

'Not you,' he said, with even more irritating confidence. 'You're steady and sensible and your values are rock-solid. All your life you've learnt to be careful with money and suspicious of superficial trappings. Those are qualities I admire and respect, Sophia.'

He was right, of course. If he'd hoped for a prudent wife, he'd chosen well. But some contrary devil in her wanted to taunt him, to make him as edgy as she'd been, to bring doubts into his mind. And what better than to suggest she'd spend, spend, spend?

'Too much scrimping and saving can make you want to break out,' she declared hotly. 'My priorities are changing. I'm beginning to enjoy the feel of beautiful fabrics against my skin, for instance. As I said earlier, designer clothes make me feel powerful. I adore them.' She allowed a little smile to play about her lips, enigmatic, enticing and deliberately hurtful. 'I intend to go on a gigantic buying spree. What's the use of a fortune if it's not enjoyed to the full?'

There was a horrible silence. Suddenly she hated herself. With apparent calm, she tilted up her chin and looked directly at him. His mouth was drawn tight, his eyes so cold that she shivered from their icy blast.

Bingo. She'd hit the spot. Her stomach churned.

'What happened to your charitable intentions?' he asked, shrivelling her with his contempt.

Sophia felt sick. In a matter of hours she'd become a mercenary shrew and her happiness had been hijacked. They'd been engaged and happy. Now they were sniping at one another. Somehow she hardened her eyes.

'I will do what I wish with my own money,' she said with a glacial stare.

She recognised the signs of his rising temper. The rock-like jaw, high shoulders, inflated chest and the utter stillness of his face, as if it were made from tempered steel.

When he spoke, however, his words were quiet and frighteningly controlled. 'You're tired. I noticed how pale you were, earlier. This has been a strain. We'll talk when you've had a rest. Remember, Sophia, that I'm the only one who knows anything about D'Antiga's affairs. Don't underestimate your need for me. You would be wise to give me your trust.'

'Trust?' she exploded. 'I wouldn't trust you to buy me an ice-cream!'

'You must!' He grabbed her arms. 'If you don't—'

'Threaten me and I'll have you thrown out!' she yelled in fury.

He went white. 'You've got it all wrong!' he grated through his teeth.

'Have I?' She was close to tears. She'd wanted him.

Loved him. And now look at them! Scrapping like kids in the playground, ready to tear one another limb from limb... His grip hadn't eased. She flashed him a scything look. 'Let go or I scream!' she hissed.

'*Sophia!*' The cry came from deep within him, a raw, visceral growl of anguish.

His mask had slipped, revealing a profound misery that shocked her to the core. He caught her face between his hands and crushed her mouth beneath his.

She tried to protest and made a feeble attempt to struggle but it convinced neither of them. In a moment his arms were around her and she was silently despairing because the feel of his body was sending thrills through her nerves. And, heaven help her, she wanted him still.

loved that. And now, hot at them. Carrying his hands in the playground, ready to run over another time from limb... Hip arm loose, sweet. She floated into a soothing look. "Eat up or I scream," she joined.

"Syrup." The words were the basis from time a vast weight away of angular.

CHAPTER SIX

SHE smelt so wonderful, tasted so good... He let his lips soften and parted them slightly so their sensitive inner surfaces could savour her heart-stopping sweetness.

Her voice whispered tremulously in his ear, imploring him unconvincingly to stop. But he couldn't. In the back of his mind he was aware that he was being indiscreet, that this was not the place or the time to give in to his overwhelming needs. No gentleman would behave so badly. But right now he didn't care. He had to touch her. Kiss her. Repair the damage that had been done.

Quickly his arm snaked out to the nearest chair, which he jammed beneath the twin door handles. And then his fingers were in her hair, gently moving over her warm scalp and releasing the elusive, tantalising perfume he associated with her. The curve of her head rested perfectly in one hand, the more voluptuous dip of her waist surrendering to the other.

And all the while his mouth moved over hers, slowly smoothing its tight anger into soft compliance. He had to obliterate her doubts. Now. Before Enrico met her.

There was a subtle change in her body—a weakening combined with a desperate urgency. And his responded, jerking with such a fierce desire and relief that he had to press her hard against him and kiss her more passionately to ease his ravenous hunger.

The soft cushions of her breasts burned through his shirt, each hard centre thrusting in erotic demand. She moaned and threw her head back. The sight of her beautiful throat and its vulnerability was too much. His mouth drifted over the silken skin with delicate, frustrating restraint.

Along her collarbone, one shoulder to the other. In the little hollow, warm, pulsing...

He shuddered as his drowsy eyes contemplated the alluring swell of her breasts above the scooped neckline. And, unable to do otherwise, he stealthily eased down her zip and bent his head to close his mouth over one turgid nipple.

She was moaning and kissing him, clutching at his shoulders in agonised pleasure. The heat in his loins became unbearable. Lifting his head to kiss her, he allowed his hand to explore her perfect breast, so soft, swollen with desire, its peak dark and throbbing beneath his fingertips.

He felt her hands tearing at his shirt buttons, sliding impatiently beneath the fabric. A groan whispered from his lips as she touched him, inexpertly—but with the instincts of a siren.

Her tongue slid around his, destroying his self-control entirely. He wanted her softness beneath him, to run his hands over her naked body, to kiss every inch and bring it to life till she was equally aroused and in need of him.

'Sophia,' he muttered roughly in her tiny ear, and he couldn't resist gently nibbling it, revelling in her answering spasm as her loins contracted. 'How I love you!'

He froze. Had he said that?

'Rozzano!' she breathed, her voice trembling with a heartbreaking sweetness.

He felt her frantic fingers fumbling for his belt. His eyes closed in a fierce attempt to gain control of himself. But already he was caressing her softly rounded hips, his hands intent on one thing only. With a groan of utter helplessness, he swung her around till her back was against the soft Fortuny fabric that clothed the wall.

His mouth tasted her breasts. Eased down her dress inch by delicious inch, the fever in his body at explosion point. Slowly he kissed and nibbled along her hipbone and across her faintly rounded stomach. She gasped and cried, her hands grasping at his hair in desperation, her legs trembling as he touched and caressed his way to the soft moistness which lay waiting for him.

'Oh, please, please!' she begged, when he hesitated.

She was beautiful. His eyes devoured her hungrily. Her eyes were almost black and gleaming with desire. Her lips were parted, red and swollen, sweetly soft against her gleaming white teeth. As she panted with need, the high, firm globes of her breasts lifted and jutted out for his touch. A faint film of sweat slicked her body, giving its curves a silvery shimmer of such beauty that he felt choked.

A strange emotion filled his head. Something beyond the physical. A kind of…joyous soaring. He dragged in a ragged breath, shaken by its intensity.

'My lovely Sophia!' he whispered thickly.

And his tongue curled around her sweetness and he felt as if he were entering paradise.

She lay later, trembling in his arms, her mind a blank— a delicious languor which kept all thoughts at bay and allowed her to bask in the wonderful sensations curling through her entire nervous system.

He loved her.

She felt like a goddess. Even now, sated and content, he was running his hands gently over her body and marvelling over it in a sleepy murmur which pulled at her heartstrings.

They sprawled on a huge damask couch and she could hear the sounds of life going on outside: a waterman's cry, a child laughing, the roar of a reversing boat engine and the ever-present lapping of the silky green water against the palace walls. Sun streamed in on them, warming her body deliciously.

She touched him in wonder. He was such a beautiful pale gold, his chest well toned and powerful. Lightly she ran her fingers down to his hard stomach. And coloured up at what that did to him.

'You blush now, after making love to me?' he teased gently.

She couldn't look at him. She would never have believed that she could have kissed away his hunger with such wanton abandon. A little shudder rippled through her. His reaction had been incredible. She'd made him groan and beg, cry aloud in hoarse longing. And his exquisite paroxysms as he'd reached his climax had been echoed inside her as her own body—inflamed by her love for him—had responded to his pleasure.

She had wanted more. They had both ached for the final union. But Rozzano had restrained his own passion and with words and gentling kisses he had calmed her, reminding her that she longed to be a virgin on her wedding night.

'I love you!' she whispered.

His mouth covered hers and he touched her again. She felt her head empty, her body become fluid as his fingers teased and tormented. This time her climax was prolonged—one deep, mind-blowing pinnacle of emotion after another.

And then she quivered in the circle of his arms again, refusing to think about anything but the feel of his heart thudding against hers, the softness of his hair beneath her fingers and the deep peace of her body.

Over the course of the next week, she fell more deeply in love. Each morning, he worked with her in the magnificent library, their voices muffled by the richly bound books lining the walls and the priceless carpet beneath their feet. They sat at their antique desks opposite one another—just as Queen Victoria had faced her beloved Albert.

With great patience, Rozzano guided her through the complexities of the D'Antiga portfolio and explained how he had managed—and increased—the family wealth. Gradually she began to realise how hard he must have worked to achieve this. And to her delight she discovered that he had donated a good deal of money to charities, particularly for the elderly and the very young.

Now, cool and elegant in a cream embroidered camisole and matching jacket, with coffee silk trousers, she hurried to the library after lunching alone with her grandfather. The previous night, Rozzano had flown to Milan for a meeting with his brother and she had been astounded by how much she'd missed him.

She waited impatiently, pacing up and down, checking her watch. He'd phoned her to say he was on the launch, that he'd be there very soon, and to wait in the library because he couldn't pretend to greet her politely and he wanted to kiss her breathless.

Her heartbeat clamoured in her breast as she heard footsteps outside. She whirled to face the door. And there he was.

Hungrily her loving eyes took in every detail: the tenderness in his face as his glance caressed every inch of her body, the immaculate Milanese suit, its severe charcoal colour relieved by a fine white stripe. The very perfection of him.

For several heart-stopping moments they gazed at one another and then he strode forward, enveloping her in his embrace.

'I've missed you!' he whispered in her ear. And he proceeded to prove that.

'Rozzano!' she protested feebly, when it seemed he was intent on stripping her. 'Later! We have so much to do! Wedding plans, our afternoon explorations of Venice—oh, I've loved seeing the city.'

'I just...needed to touch you,' he said shakily.

She smiled and wondered if he needed reassurance too. 'I want to touch you all the time,' she admitted.

'Then... How's your grandfather?' he asked eagerly.

'Very well,' she said, surprised by his manner. 'I think he's improving every day—'

'Let's tell him, Sophia!' he urged, his eyes dark and shining. 'Just him, no one else. He'll be so pleased. He adores you—'

'And he adores you.' When he began to kiss her again, she pushed him away, laughing. 'I give in!'

'He'll be having his siesta now, so...when he wakes—before we go out,' he persisted.

His enthusiasm was disarming. 'All right, Rozzano!' she said, pretending to sigh heavily. He chuckled and wandered over to his desk. 'To be honest,' she said, coming to perch on it, 'I did wonder if he'd put two and two together about us. He kept asking leading questions. So I diverted him and made him tell me about my mother.'

Rozzano leant back in his chair. 'I hope you both cleared the air.'

'I don't bear grudges.' She fiddled with her new diamond watch. 'He doesn't know why she didn't return and claim her inheritance, only that she'd sworn never to put her trust in the material world ever again.'

'Quite a sacrifice,' he commented, his eyes watchful.

'I think she was happier with Father than she was here. I feel sad for the life she led. It seems she never knew who her true friends were, and which of them were after her money—'

'It's a problem,' he said gently, his steady gaze never wavering from her face.

'I can understand that. She complained that she was expected to pay for everything. People envied and resented her. And she had two disastrous love affairs. Her lovers only wanted the lifestyle she could give them. That's when Grandfather urged her to marry your father. He thought he could save her heartache by giving her security. She felt undervalued as a person, Rozzano. That's why she gave up everything for Father, who hadn't a clue who she was until she told him on the plane to England. It must be terrible to be wanted for your money.'

'Come here, sweetheart,' he murmured, seeing her distress. Drawing her onto his knee, he cuddled her closely. 'I've had my share of gold-diggers and hangers-on. Wealth can be a barrier. It attracts greed. Sometimes those who have it become selfish and shallow because they don't need to fight and struggle in life. They get lazy and search for more and more outrageous ways to enliven their empty lives. That's why I want to protect you,' he said, kissing her temple. 'Keep you safe. You're too precious to me for anyone to spoil.'

She coiled her arms around his neck and kissed him. 'Thank you,' she said simply, ashamed that she'd ever doubted him. 'I'm glad I met you and not some poverty-stricken charmer, or a playboy hell-bent on using me as a wallet!'

'Sure.' A little abruptly, he pushed her off his lap. 'Shall we get down to work?'

'Tell me first, how was your brother?'

'Oh, in fine spirits as usual.' After a brief hesitation, he said, 'We came back on the same plane. He's arranged a surprise welcome party for you.'

She beamed. 'Great! When?'

'Tonight.' He frowned. 'Short notice. I'm not sure we can—'

'We must!' she insisted. 'He must have gone to a great deal of trouble. Besides, we're not doing anything else. Not,' she said with a wicked look, 'until *much* later tonight.'

'I would have preferred to have gone to bed early,' Rozzano said.

Sophia smiled in pleasure because he'd sounded curt, as if he was trying to control his hunger. 'I know. But think of the anticipation!' she murmured, her senses alive with excitement even now.

'Yes.' His eyes gleamed. 'Don't be surprised if I eat you alive tonight!'

She shuddered deliciously. 'Ditto!' she breathed throatily.

'Hell.' He set his jaw. 'I must get my mind off you! OK. Wedding plans, *contessa*!' he said, suddenly all efficient, the tremor in his jaw touchingly betraying his feelings. 'Then, after breaking our news to Alberto, I'm taking you out to show you the difference between a Titian and a Tintoretto.'

She rolled her eyes. 'Heavens! You're educating me now!'

'To your desk, woman,' he growled, opening letters at

a tremendous rate. 'Before I teach you a little basic biology.'

Sophia checked her moan of desire and hastily beat a retreat, settling down to examine the acceptances from guests who'd been invited to the 'celebratory ball'.

'I've had confirmation of the flight booking from Gatwick to Venice,' Rozzano told her, punching holes in a letter and adding it to their wedding file, 'and we've now found enough launches to take everyone to my family church.'

Sophia nodded, amused that she could be so blasé now about sending a plane to collect her friends! They had decided on a ceremony in the little private church adjoining the Barsini *palazzo* because it would be easier to keep out gatecrashers. And the press.

'I'm glad we decided to come back here for the reception,' she mused. 'I'm a bit staggered by the amount and variety of food, though—'

'Leave it to the caterers, darling,' he advised. 'They have experience of this. We have eighteen hundred mouths to fill, remember.'

'I can't believe it! It seems that half of Dorset and the whole of Venice will be stuffed in here!' she said in awe. 'I get nerves just thinking—'

'Don't.' His eyes held hers steadily. 'This is our wedding. Our commitment to one another. No one else— other than your grandfather—is important.'

'That's what you think. We need your family priest too! And your brother and family.'

Rozzano frowned at the letter he had just opened. 'Mmm,' he said absently. 'By the way, we're getting short of time. We must fly to Paris to buy your lingerie. I could get us on a flight tonight—'

She laughed at his eagerness. 'Your brother's arranged a party for us, remember?'

'Yes, but his parties are ten-a-penny. We could miss it—'

'Absolutely not!' she protested. 'I'm longing to meet Enrico and his family. I want to get to know them really well.'

'Paris at midnight would be more romantic—'

'Venice at midnight is romantic enough if I'm with you,' she said tenderly.

Rozzano's face eased into a slow, loving smile. 'Stay by my side the whole evening, then,' he said huskily.

'No. People will talk. We're supposed to be acquaintances, remember?' she teased. But she was delighted that he needed her so much.

'We leave the party early and go to Paris the day after, then. Yes?'

'Try to stop me!' she cried. 'I'd love to. I need to think about my wedding dress—'

'Milan,' he said promptly. 'We'll stop off there on the way back. I'll make the arrangements.'

As she changed for Enrico's party that night, she felt as if her life had accelerated into the fast lane. Her grandfather had been thrilled with their news and as she'd gazed at his tear-filled eyes she'd known that this was the best medicine they could have devised for him.

Her love for Rozzano had been intense when he'd knelt before her grandfather to embrace him, tenderness and emotion plain to see on Rozzano's face.

He was planning a wedding for them which she would never forget. Her head whirled with it all: photographs of wonderful flower displays, table decorations, discussions about the gold dinner service and the heavy white-gold cutlery, the crystal which would need cleaning, the presents for the guests, the fabulous clothes she was to have for her trousseau...

She stopped, her expression dreamy as she listened to a sweet Venetian love song. Rozzano had asked her to listen to some music by composers who'd been born in or had lived in Venice: Vivaldi, Liszt, Rossini and Bellini. It had touched her that he'd had the tracks specially compiled for her so that she could decide on her favourites for the ceremony.

Her hands paused as they were fastening her La Perla basque. She felt so strong now, so sure of Rozzano's love. His adoration had given her a pride in herself, and she knew she could cope with the pressures of managing the estate—with his help.

Slowly she snapped the fasteners and drew on the deep lace-topped stockings that he loved. For the party she had chosen a cerise silk taffeta top with a low boat neckline and a lime silk skirt, short and straight and showing more thigh than she would normally have dared. But the woman in the exclusive designer outlet had told her sternly that everyone, but everyone, was wearing their skirt that short—and that she had the legs to carry off the style.

Rozzano hadn't seen it yet. She hugged herself, anticipating the look on his face when he did. Excitedly she tucked her feet into a pair of spindly cerise shoes and scooped up the matching full-length taffeta coat. It rustled wonderfully and would billow about her in a hugely dramatic statement of confidence.

The last touch. Enormous dangling earrings. Wow!

Perfect, subtle make-up, courtesy of a beautician who'd attended to her half an hour ago, gorgeous shiny waves tumbling in artful confusion about her shoulders, thanks to a stylist who, like the beautician, had been more than eager to attend the new *contessa*.

Carefully she walked to her grandfather's suite and said goodnight to him, touched by his extravagant compliments.

'Enjoy yourself, sweetheart. Tell me all about it in the morning, yes?'

'Promise.' She kissed him tenderly. 'I love you, Grandpa,' she said softly. 'I love you very much.'

'Sweet girl,' the old man said huskily, 'you are my greatest joy.'

Her eyes sparkling with happiness, she hurried along the galleried corridor to the salon. Taking a deep breath, she checked herself carefully, composed her face as well as she could, and pushed open the doors.

Rozzano's gasp was very, very satisfying. 'Sophia!' he cried in stupefaction. 'You look...*sensational*!'

'You look gorgeous too!' she murmured, rendered breathless by his appearance. 'I think you should wear a tux day and night. You're so handsome,' she said with a sentimental sigh. 'Oh—I forgot. I have a coat, too. Look! Is that Drama Queen or what?' she cried in glee, flinging it around her shoulders and stalking about. 'I'm ready for my close-up now, Mr de Mille!' she husked extravagantly, mimicking the fading movie star in *Sunset Boulevard*.

He laughed, though his grin faded quickly. 'It's...' He opened his hands in an expression of helplessness. 'You'll knock 'em dead! But—'

'But what?' She stopped whirling about and stared at him.

'Sophia,' he began hesitantly, 'I thought you might wear something simple, like...like that little flowery dress you had in London or—'

'Rozzano!' she scolded. 'You really are hopeless! Call yourself an Italian? OK. Venetian?' she corrected hurriedly. 'I love those dresses, but they're not for a grand party in the Barsini *palazzo*! What would your brother think?'

'That's what I'm worried about,' he said lightly. 'All the men there will flock around you and the women will hate you.'

'You're flattering me!' she scoffed. 'I'm not half as lovely as some of the women I've seen around Venice. But thanks for pretending. Come on! I'm dying to be introduced to Enrico and to dance the night away!'

She held out her hand to Rozzano, her eyes brimming with happiness.

'I love you!' he whispered, pulling her close.

'I love you too,' she breathed, staring blissfully into his blazing eyes.

'Let's stay here and make love,' he urged, sliding his hand to her breast.

'Let's party and *then* make love,' she suggested, adoring him, thrilled with his hunger. Ecstatic, she pulled away and made for the door. 'I'm going—with or without you. Decide!'

With a muttered curse under his breath, he caught her up and held out his arm. When she tucked her hand in it, she discovered how tense he was. He wanted her to himself. That was very pleasing.

He fell silent during the short journey along the Grand Canal in their private gondola. They drifted along, the water gleaming like a sheet of black satin, reflecting the lamps and braziers burning on the walls of the buildings. Occasionally a waterbus would chug by, or an elegant motor launch, but otherwise the canal was peaceful.

In the quiet of the night, Rozzano's hand stole into

hers and she imagined they could be lovers from another age as the boat skimmed beneath the fabulous palaces, their huge beamed rooms illuminated by glittering chandeliers.

'I'm in a fairy tale,' she said with a sigh. 'Once I was Cinderella and met a prince. I seem to have avoided the wicked ugly sisters!'

'Watch out for the wolf.'

'Wrong fairy tale, darling!' she said with a giggle. She leaned back against the cushions, entranced by the beauty of the canal, and gripped his hand very tightly. 'I can't believe it, Rozzano,' she confessed. 'I could burst with happiness!'

'Prefer it if you didn't,' he drawled. 'Ruin my tux.'

'We're coming to the Rialto Bridge. Which is your house?' she asked eagerly.

So far, he'd refused to show her the Barsini palace, saying they'd visit it when they had plenty of time and she could appreciate it properly.

'The one with green and gold striped awnings.'

Her eyes sparkled as they drew nearer. It was, she knew, thirteenth-century and therefore smaller, with intimate rather than grand salons. Once it had boasted its own dock, where cargoes had unloaded from Africa and the Orient—gold and silver, brocades and silks, amber and carpets.

'Next time we come here it will be our wedding day,' he said quietly.

'Surely not!' she said in surprise, as the gondolier manoeuvred the boat to the jetty. 'We're bound to be visiting your brother before then!'

'We won't have time,' he said shortly, waiting while a flunkey in velvet knee breeches carefully assisted her onto the jetty. 'Millions of things to do, Sophia.'

They walked into a hall and Sophia's first impression was that it shimmered, its ochre walls almost obliterated by gold tissue streamers and green satin ribbons. It was so packed, they could hardly move. Hundreds of people were chattering excitedly, their exotic Mediterranean colouring heightened by the glittering clothes and jewels of the women, and the sharp white tuxedos of the men.

Green and gold predominated in the stunning flower displays hanging from the coffered ceiling, the occasional frond trailing alarmingly close to a tiara or two. She inhaled the air, trying to remember some of her grandfather's teaching.

'Attar of roses—can you smell it? Jasmine. Patchouli…and…I think there's a base note of sandalwood,' she said to Rozzano, raising her voice above the noise.

'Alberto will be proud of you! The beams are sandalwood. Warmth and moisture intensify the aroma,' he replied, speaking with his mouth close to her ear.

They began to push through the packed bodies. Now she could hear the faint strains of a string quartet, playing eighteenth-century music. 'It's very lavish!' she yelled.

Rozzano grunted. 'Enrico doesn't stint himself.'

He grasped her elbow tightly and she winced. 'You're hurting!' she complained.

'I'm sorry.'

She frowned. He looked pale. People were greeting him and staring at her. He acknowledged them briefly but forged on without making introductions, pushing her up a flight of stairs and into a slightly less crowded ballroom, which glowed warmly from the light of a crystal chandelier and hundreds of candle-sconces.

'Rozzano! My dear brother!' The two men embraced and Enrico turned to her. 'So this is Sophia!' He kissed

her three times, holding her shoulders and gazing at her
with the same intent stare as Rozzano's. But his face—
although handsome—was softer, less chiselled and his
mouth a weaker version. 'But I am amazed!' Enrico murmured, turning her face this way and that. 'She's not like
a horse at all!'

Sophia giggled. 'I should hope not!'

'You described her badly,' Enrico reproached his
brother. 'She's lovely. How you could say her voice
sounded like the neigh of an old mare—?'

'OK, Enrico,' Rozzano drawled. His eyes were like
slits, belying the bland expression on his face. 'Enough
joking—'

'Joking? It's what you said!' his brother protested.
Turning indignantly to Sophia, he explained. 'I rang him
when I saw a rather indistinct picture of you in the newspaper here. He said that there was nothing between you
and, besides, you—'

'Looked like a horse.' She had managed to recover her
equilibrium, but inside she was quaking. Was that really
Rozzano's opinion? 'Excuse me,' she murmured sweetly,
desperate to put space between herself and Rozzano. 'I'm
going to graze.'

'Sophia—!'

Too choked to answer, she ignored his ground-out plea
and slipped through the crowd, ending up in another
room entirely. Immediately she was pounced on by a
group of beautiful women who looked as though they
might be models.

'You must be Sophia D'Antiga! How lovely, darling!'
The speaker—dainty and bean-thin, with wonderful bone
structure—gave Sophia the triple kiss and stared at her
in slightly drunken surprise. 'You look better than I expected! Rozzano told Enrico you were—'

'Like a horse,' she said drily, feeling like one in contrast to this diminutive vision. 'I know. He doesn't think much of me, does he? Does the whole of Venice know his opinion?'

The woman laughed prettily, and sent heavy wine fumes in Sophia's direction. 'Only family! I am Letizia, Enrico's wife. How rude Zano has been about you! We were prepared for the very *worst*! Perhaps you *are* on the large side, but not quite as unattractive and awkward as Zano said! Why, he said your clothes were appalling and your manners worse! He led us to believe that you might turn up in a home-made dress and department-store shoes! Isn't he a scream?'

'Hysterical,' she agreed, wondering grimly what *Zano* really thought of her. She didn't like Letizia much. Beneath that friendly manner was a sly determination to cut the new *contessa* down to size. 'I could go back and get my home-made dress and chain-store shoes if you like,' she offered innocently.

'You...*have* such things?' Letizia gaped. 'That's terrible! You must throw them away immediately! Darling, we *must* do the shops together,' she continued in her nasal drawl. 'Pop into Cartier's, do the Boulevard St-Germain—I need underwear, darling, and it's the only place to go—nip over to London for lunch at San Lorenzo's—their amaretto creams are *divine*—'

'I'm awfully busy,' Sophia broke in hastily. 'Trying to understand the family finances for a start and—'

'Good heavens!' Letizia exclaimed in horror. 'You can't deprive Zano of his baby! He adores playing the stockmarket. It's his passion! He's had the freedom of the D'Antiga power for some years now. What would he do without it? Let him continue. Men provide, women decorate—and spend the money. And I'm the girl to help you do that!' she chirruped, flinging up her arms theatrically and dazzling everyone with an impromptu firework display from the emeralds and diamonds around her wrists.

'At the moment,' Sophia said firmly, 'I'm arranging a huge party and that's taking up all my spare time—'

'I know, darling; entertaining does cut into one's personal freedom. I'm so busy this week that I've no idea when I'll have time to exfoliate! Here,' she said, grabbing a canapé from a liveried footman and staggering a little as she did so, 'have one of these. And,' she whispered under her breath, her eyes ogling the footman's broad back, 'isn't that man to die for?'

'Hunky,' Sophia agreed, looking at the canapé dubiously. 'What is this?'

'Foie gras, of course! Only the best. Eat it up and it'll give us an excuse to drag him back—'

'I can't eat it!' Sophia cried in outrage. 'I don't believe in force-feeding geese till their livers balloon up!'

'How terribly bourgeois!' Letizia looked down her nose at Sophia. 'Personally I never touch the stuff, but then I take care of my figure.' She cast an expert eye over Sophia's more generous curves. 'Take my advice, darling. If you want your pick of the men here, lose some weight. In the wrong clothes, you could look like a tart. Look!' she screeched suddenly. 'Zano's on the prowl for a wife! Poor darling, he's been searching for someone like Nicoletta for *ages*. I think he's found her! Lucky Arabella!'

Sophia followed Letizia's gaze. A slim wand of a woman had draped herself all over him, as if, Sophia thought waspishly, she couldn't manage to stand on her own.

'Why is Rozzano trying to find a wife?' she asked, fighting a surge of jealousy.

'He needs an heir, darling. That's the only reason these aristocratic males marry,' Letizia said bitterly, knocking back a huge goblet of wine. 'They can have any woman they want, so they play around till they realise they must produce children for the sake of the family.'

'Is that what Rozzano's been doing? Playing the field?' Sophia asked quietly. And jealousy coiled in her stomach. Of course he would have had relationships. He was too passionate to hold his drive in check. Her eyes flickered with pain.

'Who knows? He's too secretive. But Arabella's ideal for a wife. English, but she's terribly rich and blue-blooded. Family goes back to the Middle Ages.'

'I imagine everyone's family must,' Sophia observed drily.

Her observation was lost on Letizia. 'She's my best friend. She's been renting a *palazzo* ever since she came to the Carnival and fell in love with Venice. I'd better warn her.'

Sophia stiffened. 'About what?'

'Marriage to a Venetian noble. They hate losing their freedom. In a fit of temper and duty they marry and then keep mistresses to amuse them. Wives are baby machines, Sophia,' she added with telling venom. 'Take my advice. Marry a poor man. He'll be after your money, but at least he won't expect a child a year after your marriage, or run after every pretty woman who crosses his path!'

Sophia sensed Letizia was talking of her own marriage. Although she didn't like the woman, she pitied her for feeling so unloved.

'Rozzano doesn't seem the way you describe...' she began hesitantly.

Letizia sniffed elegantly. 'Oh, but he is! He'll marry for power and wealth as they all do. These places cost a fortune to run. One thing is certain: he'll never love another woman. Nicoletta was his great passion. Poor Enrico was *petrified* when she died.'

Sophia frowned, trying to follow the woman's ramblings. 'Enrico? Why?'

'We thought Zano might commit suicide. Think of the shame on the family name!' Letizia cried in horror.

'It would have been awful for you to cope with the shame,' Sophia acknowledged, without even a hint of the contempt she felt for Rozzano's sister-in-law.

'Well, that's Zano for you. Selfish like all men. No, he'll marry someone suitable, get a handful of children and then sneak away for sex elsewhere. They get used to variety and hate giving it up. Why should they, when so many women are willing to oblige?'

Why indeed. The colours in the room swam before Sophia's eyes, the laughter, gossip and music merging in one mind-numbing noise. Letizia continued sounding off and swaying, but Sophia paid no attention.

Dimly she saw Rozzano enter the room. Arabella was still brilliantly impersonating a shawl over his arm and shoulder and snuggling up with cosy familiarity. It upset her that he seemed perfectly at home with these shallow people. He was a little distant, perhaps, but urbane and courteous.

Sophia watched him, her eyes wounded. Letizia had been so certain of his motives and intentions—and she must know him well. Again the importance of the family had come to the fore. Rozzano *did* want children—as quickly as possible. Was she to be a baby machine too, then abandoned when boredom set in?

Nausea rose, vile and uncontrollable, to her throat, and she muttered an excuse, hurrying to the powder room which had been pointed out to her when they'd arrived. It was very grand, with gold taps, buckets of ice containing champagne and mineral water, and enormous foxtail lilies everywhere, their sickly perfume making her feel worse.

She sipped some water till the nausea subsided then took several deep breaths and fought for calm again. Rozzano must have joked about her looking like a horse. It was the kind of thing one brother might say to another. She steadied herself. He'd said he loved her.

But then he would, wouldn't he?

Her lips pressed hard together. He did care; it was there in his eyes for her to see. And he couldn't have faked his desire, or his lovemaking...

Unless he'd been desperate. And he was a man, for whom sex could be divorced from love.

Pale and shaking, she gripped the edge of the basin. He loves me, she told herself. He loves me.

Although I look like a horse and don't have a size eight figure like Arabella. Even though we've only just met. Even though he adores the D'Antiga house and would obviously hate to move back into the Barsini palace.

Who was she trying to kid?

She stared at her white face in the rococo mirror, her dark eyes and the slash of cerise lipstick a stark contrast to the alabaster of her skin. She wasn't beautiful. More like a fool. A sow's ear in a silk purse.

Anger flowed, hot and souring in her stomach. She wanted to be loved for herself. And for no other reason.

She tidied herself up, smiled with brittle sharpness at

her reflection and sallied forth to spend the evening chatting to the least unpleasant of Enrico's friends: Russian aristocrats in tiaras and velvets, counts and princes in exquisite silk tuxedos and English gentry in their pearls and cameos.

Aristocrats were actually in the minority. Most of Enrico's guests seemed to be minor celebrities, models and footballers—people who appeared on the front pages of tabloids and in gossip columns. And the atmosphere was heavy with spiteful gossip, with intrigue and open flirtations being the norm.

The champagne flowed, the music swirled, and her head ached and screamed for solitude. But that was the one thing she didn't want because she'd be forced to think about her future. So she stuck it out, even when the sight of various couples avidly exploring one another's bodies made her turn away in disgust.

If this was the kind of behaviour Rozzano condoned, they'd find it impossible to live together. Her misery deepened as the party became more raucous and alcohol released the guests from any remaining inhibitions.

Sometimes she saw Rozzano's head above the throng. But he studiously ignored her—and she him. Much of the time Arabella seemed to be at his side, and Sophia wondered uncharitably if Rozzano enjoyed being eyed as if he were a god made mortal.

Why not? a nasty little voice said inside her head. Men loved to be flattered. Arabella was certainly doing that, with her doe eyes and submissive body language. Sophia scowled.

'Dance, Sophia?'

When she turned, she almost collided with Enrico's muscular chest. Something about him made her want to recoil, but she knew it would be bad manners to refuse.

'Thank you,' she said politely.

There was a commotion behind her and suddenly Rozzano's hand was on her shoulder.

'Sorry, Rico, but I have to take Sophia back,' he said pleasantly. 'She's not used to staying up late. Gets sick if she eats rich food and drinks alcohol.'

Sophia's eyes narrowed at his blatant untruths. Now why was he trying to stop her from spending time with his brother?

'She'll be all right with me,' Enrico murmured, his eyes glittering hungrily.

'She's up early for her Italian lesson,' Rozzano insisted, steel lacing his silken voice.

That was news to her. 'Am I?' she asked, frowning, toying with the idea of quizzing Enrico while they danced.

'You're learning the parts of the body. Head, nose, arms...'

She glared, reading the message in his half-veiled eyes. He intended to give her a hands-on lesson!

'I can teach her more interesting words than that.' Enrico's gaze was significantly glued to her bosom. He slipped his arm around Sophia's waist and pressed his hip hard against hers.

Suddenly she became horribly aware of his sexual interest in her. His scent was overpowering, his pheromones even more so.

'I'm afraid Rozzano is right. I'd better go,' she said quickly, glad of an excuse to escape. Her hand went to her mouth in mock dismay. 'Heavens! I think I'm going to throw up any moment!'

Enrico jumped away in alarm and in grim satisfaction she slipped through the crowd with Rozzano hard on her heels, grateful to be leaving the party at last.

'Well done. Thought we'd never get away,' he said with satisfaction.

'Really? Why did you turn up just when Enrico asked me to dance?' she asked coolly when they emerged from the watergate and walked to the waiting gondola.

'I wanted to get you away from him,' he replied easily. 'He flirts when he's had a glass or two of wine.'

Or a bucket of it, she thought uncharitably. 'So you were jealous.'

'I suppose so. Do you find him attractive?'

What should she say? That she found most of the people there not to her taste—but Enrico actually made her skin crawl?

'I could tease you and pretend that I do,' she said after a while. 'But that would be a lie. I didn't want to dance with him. To be honest, I didn't enjoy myself much,' she added quietly, omitting to explain that the revelation about Rozzano would have ruined even a wonderful evening.

He grimaced. 'I'd had enough too. Sophia...they were Enrico's friends, not mine. You've met one or two of my friends over lunch and you said you liked them. I think you'll like the rest of them, too. They're not...'

'Flash?' she provided wryly, and he gave a small laugh and nodded. 'You don't like his friends.'

'Not much.'

Relieved at that, she gave him a shrewd glance. 'You don't like your brother much either, do you?'

'He is my brother.' Rozzano's expression gave nothing away. 'I am responsible for him.'

'You evaded my question. And you're not your brother's keeper. He's an adult. Whatever role you had to play in his life in the past, it's over now.'

'He is a Barsini,' he said obstinately. 'Whatever he does reflects on my family.'

'And family is all,' she said in a small voice, her heart chilling when he made no answer.

Her disapproval made him clam up, his jaws jammed together obstinately. She stared ahead sightlessly, her senses dulled, all the joy gone from her life. Family. Family. *Family*! It couldn't be more important than love and honesty and kindness to others. It shouldn't be a barrier to happiness, or to truth.

She must know one way or the other. Either Rozzano loved her—*her*, not her title, her inheritance, her suitability—or he was putting his wretched dynasty before his own feelings.

Numbly she walked up to her suite, her legs barely holding her up.

'Come in,' she said in a low whisper.

'You don't look as if you're in the mood,' he said, frowning.

She flung her head up, her eyes anguished. 'I'm not. There's something I must ask you. Come in.'

The door closed quietly behind him. She swallowed, not knowing what she would do if he admitted the truth. A terrible sickness engulfed her again and she hurried over to pour herself a glass of mineral water, her shoulders heaving convulsively as she struggled to control her misery.

'Enrico said something to you, didn't he? What was it?' Rozzano asked in a menacing tone.

She'd been right. He feared any contact she might make with his brother. What would Enrico tell her, given half the chance? Swinging around, her cerise cloak billowing out behind her, she met his wary eyes and felt a shaft of fear strike her heart.

'I hardly spoke to him.' She noticed his exhalation of relief and trembled. 'But I heard things that made me doubt you, Rozzano.'

'From whom?' he demanded grimly.

'It doesn't matter. But I want you to answer me truthfully,' she said, her eyes fixed steadily on his. Her hands plucked nervously at her waistband. 'No lies, Rozzano. Be honest. Do you really love me?' she cried, her raised chin and determined mouth defying him to deceive her. 'Would you love me if I gave all my money away and if I was plain Sophia Charlton in a home-made dress and with no D'Antiga blood at all?'

The affection in his face gave her the answer straight away. 'Is that what's been worrying you, sweetheart? My darling, how can you ask?'

Tenderly he smiled at her, the love in his eyes warming her cold body through and through, bringing life to her icy heart and dulled brain.

'I really love you,' he said gently. 'Give your wealth away if you must. This palace, even. I would still want to live with you for the rest of my life.'

It was what she'd wanted to hear. Without hesitation she ran to his arms, sobbing. And he stroked her back gently, his cheek against hers.

'You must never distrust me, no matter what rumours you hear,' he whispered. 'Enrico's friends love nothing better than to gossip and to pull people apart. They spread lies for sheer amusement.'

'I can believe that,' she said earnestly.

'Have faith in me, Sophia,' he murmured adoringly. 'I mean to cherish you to the end of my days. But... especially tonight!'

And that still September night there *was* something very different about their lovemaking. It was slower, more lingering and languid yet with deeper resonances which reached far into the core of her.

Rozzano loved her with all his heart. She could sleep in peace. There was no doubt in her mind at all.

CHAPTER SEVEN

DRESSED in his morning suit and embroidered waistcoat, he waited far above the Grand Canal, his heart pounding unnaturally. He had climbed out onto the *altana*, the small platform on the roof of Ca' Barsini. Here, medieval princesses of his family had once fanned out their waist-length hair to bleach it in the sun.

But today he was waiting for his princess bride to appear. He knew he shouldn't be there, that he ought to be welcoming their guests, but he'd felt compelled to make absolutely certain that she hadn't changed her mind.

A terrible fear clutched at his loins. She was late. She must come! Suppose… God! Suppose she'd heard a rumour? Despite all his plans to keep them apart, Enrico might have got to her somehow and poisoned her mind.

More nervous than he'd ever been in the whole of his life, he shaded his eyes against the low autumn sun, willing her to come into view. His hands held the rail in a fierce grip as he stared tensely at the bend of the canal, around which she should have appeared. If she was coming.

He heard something. Hooters. Sirens, a faint cheer… Sharply he drew in his breath and didn't release it until the small convoy of boats came into sight.

'Thank God!' he whispered, utterly shaken by the relief that washed through his body. Craning his neck forward, he leaned out for a better view.

She sat opposite Alberto in the gondola, the skirts of her dress spread all around her and emphasising her tiny waist. She wore his wedding present: a priceless baroque pearl hanging from a pearl necklace.

Rozzano's eyes kindled. The neckline above her slender-fitting bodice was deep, displaying her beautiful shoulders and the faint dark line of her cleavage.

Beneath the veil her face was indistinct, but he caught the occasional flash of her teeth as she waved happily to the boatmen who had spotted their favourite sight—a Venetian bride—and had joined in the procession.

He grinned exultantly. She'd be his, in less than an hour! He'd dreamed of this moment; worked and schemed to achieve it. This was his reward.

Closing his eyes in satisfaction, he threw back his head and inhaled the mixture of salt and marsh, roses and diesel that was essentially Venice. Gently he eased out his breath and with it all the tensions of the past few years. At last he had everything he could wish for!

Quite extraordinarily elated, he hurried back to organise the transfer of their guests from the ballroom to the adjoining family church. Then with enormous satisfaction, he ushered his bewildered brother to the front pew, to stand beside him.

'Why are we in church? What the hell's going on?' complained Enrico.

'Wait and see,' Rozzano drawled, barely able to contain his excitement.

The music soared. Sophia must be outside, he thought, his hands suddenly clammy. He directed his brother's attention to the two coats of arms beneath the lavish flower display by the altar. As was the custom for a Barsini marriage, the Barsini coat of arms had been positioned next to those of the bride with silk ribbons in the D'Antiga blue and white twining around the Barsini hues of green and gold.

'My…God!' The truth was clearly beginning to dawn on Enrico.

'Remain calm, brother,' Rozzano purred.

'Sophia? But you—you don't like her!'

'Is that relevant? This is for the good of the family,' he said sardonically. 'I need children. Here's the ring. Don't lose it.'

Enrico was speechless. Rozzano smiled in triumph.

There was one more thing that would make the day complete. His eyes gleamed. Arabella. He would see her privately, during the reception.

'No, your sleeves are fine.'

Sophia's bridesmaids—friends she'd known all her life—firmly prevented her from heaving up the pearl-encrusted neckline, and pushed it down again so that the little cap sleeves sat off the shoulder.

She stared at the bodice doubtfully. She loved the little daisies formed by the clusters of seed-pearls but felt alarmed by the amount of cleavage she was showing.

'It's a bit daring—' she began.

'You look fantastic. Leave well alone!' said Maggie sternly. She began to fuss with Sophia's hair, making sure the pins holding Sophia's smooth Grace Kelly-style chignon were firmly in place.

'We can't improve you any more, sadly. Turn around and let us do our job!' teased Jenny. 'It's *molto tardi*! That means late. And we don't have a *disco orario*! A parking ticket to you plebs,' she added with mock scorn.

'OK, clever. I'd forgotten you majored in Italian and French!' she grumbled, but obeyed.

This was it! Her knees trembled with nerves as they lifted the heavy train, which was deeply scalloped and lavishly embroidered with pearls. The music filled her head with sound, its sweet notes bringing a lump to her throat.

'Wagons roll!' Maggie called from some way behind her.

She chuckled and felt her nerves melt away. Her friends had been wonderful. They had kept her secret, despite their excitement at being flown to Paris for dress fittings.

Turning, she smiled with affection at the two girls. They looked lovely. The buttermilk colour of the simple but chic ballgown dresses really flattered their dark colouring.

'Are you ready, sweetheart? They're playing your music!' her grandfather said fondly.

'I'm ready,' she replied, husky with emotion.

His valet helped him from the little gilt chair where he had been waiting, smoothed down her grandfather's coat tails and handed him his stick. He leant on Sophia's arm.

Carefully she positioned her bouquet of sweetly perfumed cabbage roses then waited expectantly while the church doors were flung open by two of Rozzano's grinning house staff.

Faces turned, mouths opened. Sophia fought back a grin at everyone's astonishment as heads swivelled back to where Rozzano stood, tall and erect, at the far end of the church. Judging by the buzz of chatter, only the few they'd sworn to secrecy had known the true purpose of the celebratory party!

Slowly she and her grandfather progressed down the aisle. She felt overjoyed that he'd been well enough to give her away. In fact, his health had improved enormously. Somehow her pending marriage to Rozzano had given him a new lease of life.

Shyly she met the eyes of the man she loved above all

others. From then until the moment he placed the ring on her finger at the end of the simple ceremony, they hardly looked away from one another.

Throughout the ceremony, her senses were so highly tuned that she was acutely aware of everything around her—the dignity of her proud grandfather, the hush when a choirboy sang 'Pié Jésu' with agonising sweetness, the catch in Rozzano's voice when he spoke his vows.

She couldn't join in with the hymns because her heart was too full. Instead, she stood quietly, awed by the unexpectedness of love that had brought her here.

And she felt so serene that she even smiled understandingly when Enrico failed to hand over the ring. Rozzano muttered something under his breath and his brother responded.

Blissfully Sophia raised her face to her lover as he lifted her veil and kissed her tenderly, his mouth lingering softly on hers while his eyes promised her the world.

Man and wife, she thought dreamily. Man and wife.

When they paused in the courtyard for photographs, they were both swamped by people hugging and kissing them. Everyone seemed warm and friendly—and genuinely delighted by the surprise wedding. Sophia felt a vast sense of relief that Rozzano's friends were very different from Enrico's.

'Well, you *are* a dark horse,' Letizia murmured nastily in Sophia's ear. 'You didn't take any notice of what I said, did you? Enjoy it while you can. He'll stray. It's bred in the blood. Just watch out for Arabella. That's my wedding gift to you.'

'I'm sorry you're so unhappy,' Sophia began gently.

'Me? I live in a palace, I can spend what I want—are you mad?'

Sophia bit her lip, sad to see such misery on her wedding day.

'The boats are ready, darling! Let me lift you in!' cried Rozzano, appearing at her side.

Laughing and protesting at the extra weight of her sumptuous dress, she challenged him to do so. Carefully he set her on the cushions of his palatial launch and soon they were moving off at the head of a slow convoy. Police boats, acting as outriders, activated their blue flashing lights and yelled through megaphones to warn the frantic paparazzi to keep clear.

The exuberant Mario had embraced them both tearfully before taking the wheel. Suddenly he burst into spontaneous song, his glorious tenor voice echoing from the high walls of the palaces. Soon the refrain had spread through the convoy till almost everyone was singing with him.

Sophia hugged herself in delight. Looking back, she saw that they'd picked up a whole fleet of barges and motorboats, some *sandoli*, *vaporetti*, gondolas, and...

'Look, Rozzano! A refuse boat! Can't see any vests or tattoos, though,' she said.

He rolled his eyes. 'One of these days I fear I'll lose you to some dustman,' he complained.

'Never. You're not getting rid of me that easily.'

He kissed her to a chorus of cheers. 'Good,' he murmured. And kissed her again.

'I've never been happier,' she said with a contented sigh.

'Wait till our first child is born!' he teased.

A flicker of nerves subdued her for a moment and she gazed at him warily. 'What if I can't have children, Rozzano?' she asked anxiously.

'Don't even think of it,' he murmured, devouring her mouth with a deep, intimate kiss.

But she did. He wanted an heir very badly. If she couldn't provide one...

The nagging worry wouldn't go away. It stayed with her, spoiling the wonderful reception. Sipping a Bellini and nibbling the occasional bite-sized savoury *cicchetti*, she happily accepted the kisses and congratulations from her friends and his. She even enjoyed the faces of the children when the stilt-walkers and fire-eaters appeared. But the fear remained like a spectre at a feast.

'Hello, Frank! And Mrs Luscombe... Thank you for coming!' she cried, pleased to see the man who'd first brought the two of them together.

'So glad,' Frank said warmly. 'I thought there was something between you two, right from the start!'

Sophia went pink and the Luscombes laughed.

'We had an amazing trip over,' Frank's wife marvelled. 'Two coachloads of us. We stayed in a swanky hotel in London and were swept in a fleet of motorboats to stay at the Danieli! It's like a dream. What it must be like for you, I don't know! But you have a gem there, Sophia. Look—he's got the woman from our post office eating out of his hands! And you should have seen the way he listened solemnly to some maid telling him—so Jenny said, because we didn't understand a word of course—how to stay happily married!'

Sophia giggled. 'That'll be Flavia! All his staff have been with his family for generations. They believe they have a vested interest in keeping him on the straight and narrow!'

'Well, I don't think you'll have any trouble there,' Frank said. 'And I've had years of assessing people's characters. There! He's heading for those children. See the look on his face? You can see how soft he is inside, despite that air of authority.'

'Yes,' she said tenderly. 'I can.'

From the way his friends' children flung themselves at him with shrieks of delight, he was evidently a favourite. From her own experience she could see how natural he was with them and there was no doubt that he genuinely adored children.

It would be a double tragedy for him if they didn't have any. No immediate heir to the Barsini-D'Antiga estates, no child of their own to love. Her eyes darkened. It would put an intolerable strain on their marriage.

'Look at him! Typical. He has all the fun, none of the responsibility,' came Letizia's sour voice from behind her. 'You'll be the one to get fat and ugly every time you produce one of his brats. *He'll* still look the same— handsome and charming. Woman bait.'

Sophia ignored Letizia's bitter words, watching as he extricated himself from the laughing children, made some kind of promise, and swept a hand over his tousled hair. His face was relaxed and glowing with happiness. Accepting a glass of Krug from one of his servants, he searched the room for her.

She was about to raise an arm to catch his attention when he apparently saw the person he'd been seeking and began determinedly making his way through the chattering guests. In the opposite direction.

Her spirits fell. He hadn't been looking for her, after all.

'Arabella,' Letizia said cynically. 'I might have guessed.'

'What makes you think that? I can't see her,' Sophia said haughtily.

'Neither can he. She's just left the room by the far door. He'll go after her in a moment.'

It did seem as if she was right. Sophia took a hasty gulp of her Bellini, refusing to be upset by Letizia's innuendo.

'You're wrong. He's not interested in her,' she said coolly, as he disappeared into the next *salotto*.

'Prove it. Find him, you'll find her,' sneered Letizia.

'I trust him. He loves me,' Sophia countered, angry with the woman for being so malicious.

'He had one love only in his life, and she died,' Letizia said nastily. 'He wouldn't risk his heart a second time. He was brought up to deny his feelings. Enrico told me that his father would rap them both on the knuckles if they showed emotion in public. Their mother hardly saw them. She partied all night and slept all day. Neither Rico nor Zano will surrender to love. They have the Barsini coat of arms where most men have hearts!'

'No, Letizia, you're wrong,' she said angrily. 'Whatever Enrico's faults, Rozzano does know how to love—'

'Oh, he's a great *lover*,' sneered Letizia. 'He has a reputation for that.'

'I won't listen to this any longer!' Sophia seethed. 'I'll prove you're wrong!' And, fuming, she hurried to catch him up.

Letizia was mistaken—it was only her twisted mind that saw desire where none existed. Rozzano wasn't a two-timer. Everyone here adored him. He couldn't possibly fool all these clever and perceptive people.

He was wonderful. The best. Kind, good, hard working and a fabulous lover. There wasn't a treacherous bone in his body.

Yet her knees knocked together as she followed

Rozzano's trail, blushing at the teasing she encountered whenever she asked where he'd gone.

Suddenly she was alone, in an empty corridor. And she could hear the raised voices of a man and a woman coming from behind one of the doors. A horrible coldness invaded her body. Folding her arms around her for comfort, she tiptoed closer to the source of the sound.

'Oh, thank goodness it's you, Sophia!' came Jenny's relieved voice from behind her.

Sophia spun around in embarrassment. 'What's the matter?' she asked nervously.

'I'm lost. Went to find the loo and this is where I ended up— Hey, who's that yelling?'

'Could be anyone,' Sophia said uncomfortably, knowing Rozzano's voice far too well. It was obvious that he'd totally lost his temper. She'd never heard his native tongue sound so brutal. Panicking, she said, 'Jenny, this doesn't concern us. I think we'd better go—'

'Good grief!' Jenny blanched, a look of horror spreading over her face. 'Oh, Sophia!' she gasped, her hand clapped to her mouth.

Feeling sick, Sophia steadied herself against the doorjamb while Rozzano continued to vent his spleen and Jenny's eyes grew rounder and rounder.

Her spirits sank. She'd known he had a violent temper, which he'd kept from her very successfully. What else had he managed to hide?

'What is it?' she demanded in a hoarse whisper.

'N-nothing! Better go as you said—'

'You've heard something awful! I know it!'

Jenny looked panic-stricken. 'Don't ask, Sophia!' she begged.

'You must tell me!' She caught Jenny's shoulders in

a firm grip, her eyes bright with unshed tears. 'You must tell me! You're my friend,' she muttered fiercely.

Jenny continued to stare at her in mute dismay and Sophia gritted her teeth. 'I can't!' her friend said eventually.

'You owe me this!' hissed Sophia. 'We started school together. I untied you from the bike shed. You and Maggie stopped that bully picking on me. I warned you about that awful Jack Spencer. We did everything together till you went off to university. Don't let me down, Jenny! Tell me what he's so angry about!'

Jenny chewed her lip. 'I swear, you don't want to know—'

'I do,' Sophia said bleakly. 'Can't you see? I know something's wrong and it'll eat away at me until I find out!'

Her friend's head drooped and she mumbled, 'You'll wish you never asked.'

'But I am asking. So give!'

Jenny's eyes filled with tears. 'It's…Rozzano. He was yelling that… Oh, God! That he—he married you to get an heir. That he doesn't love you and never will. Sophia, I—!'

'No!' Horrified, she shrank from her friend's outstretched arms. 'Leave me, Jenny,' she whispered, her face a mask of ice. 'Thank you for telling me. I prefer to know the truth.' Suddenly she felt numb, almost paralysed with shock. 'Don't tell anyone, not even Maggie.' Her agonised eyes met Jenny's. 'Please do this for me!'

'Sophia…' Jenny began brokenly.

'No!' she breathed, stepping back, her eyes wide with alarm. No sympathy. Or she'd disintegrate. 'I'm OK,' she said quietly, only a faint tremor in her voice. 'Please go. I have to have this out with him and whoever's in there.'

She waited till her friend had fled in tears. A stubborn pride was holding her up and her muscles were so rigid that she could only move jerkily towards the door like a clockwork doll. Before she could reach the handle however, the door flew open and to her surprise Enrico came hurtling out.

White-faced and shaking like a leaf, he closed the door behind him. 'Sophia!' he said in sharp shock.

'What were you doing in there?' she asked in bewilderment.

'I—I…' He licked his lips, seemingly struck dumb.

'I know Rozzano's in there!' she declared in an undertone. 'I heard him! Don't try to cover up for him. What's he doing, Enrico? Who's he with?'

Enrico's eyes narrowed slyly. 'I was…er…having a word with him. I—I thought he ought to be with his guests, with you and…not anyone else.' Enrico's laboured explanation suddenly gathered speed as if he was more confident. 'He shouted at me because I interrupted him in the middle of—'

'All right!' She'd got the picture. She didn't want diagrams. 'Let me pass,' she whispered, white-lipped.

'You can't go in there—' he blustered.

'Let me pass!' she repeated hysterically through her teeth.

Enrico shrugged. 'If you must.' He gave her a pitying look. 'I did what I could, Sophia. I suppose you have a right to know what he does on his wedding day.'

Sophia gulped. Her legs were shaking so much she hardly knew how she would stay upright. 'Exactly. Move aside.'

'Why don't you take a little look without him knowing? Allow me.' With an expression of great concern, he silently opened the door a fraction and beckoned her to the narrow gap.

Her heart in her mouth, she peered into the room. And her world fell apart.

Rozzano had his back to her. He was handing a pair of stockings to Arabella, who wore only a sexy red basque and briefs, her dress having been hastily discarded in a scarlet pool of soft silk on the carpet.

Sophia's eyes closed in utter despair. For several seconds nothing happened inside her. The extent of his betrayal had left her unable to breathe or move or speak.

Then her brain whirred into life, torturing her, telling her that everything between them had been a lie. The tender glances, the courtship, the passionate declarations of love...

Stifling a sob, she finally managed to turn away just as Arabella was reaching a hand around Rozzano's waist. She had no wish to witness his actual infidelity. Quietly Enrico closed the door. With a taste of bile in her mouth, she let him help her to the far end of the corridor where she collapsed weakly on a settle.

Wanting to scream, she pushed the knuckles of her clenched fist into her mouth and sank her teeth into her hand. He'd made a fool of her, over and over again! He'd persuaded her to marry him when he knew what marriage meant to her, how sacred, how special it was! She couldn't believe anyone could be so beautiful and plausible and yet be utterly rotten and *poisonous* underneath!

'I'm sorry,' Enrico said silkily, pawing her arm. 'I did my best but everyone thinks he's some kind of demi-god—'

'I know, and more fool us!' Her eyes flashed as hard and as brilliant as diamonds. 'Don't tell him I was here,' she warned Enrico vehemently. 'I don't want him to know. Yet.'

'No, no,' he promised eagerly. 'It'll be our secret.'

'And don't tell anyone else, either,' she muttered through her teeth. 'If my grandfather hears, he could die of shock.' In her passion she grabbed Enrico's lapels and thrust her face near to his. 'Do you understand that, Enrico? No gossip, not a word, a hint of this, or by God you'll regret you ever lived!'

'Not a word!' he squeaked in terror. She released him and he whined, 'What are you going to do, Sophia?'

Her chin lifted with cold pride. Rozzano had taken her dreams and trampled on them. He deserved to be in hell.

'That's simple. Ruin his plans,' she said venomously.

CHAPTER EIGHT

HER anger sustained her through the banquet, although every second was an ordeal. She had decided it was vital that Rozzano suspected nothing until she was ready to tell him in private. How could she ruin the day for her blissfully happy grandfather?

Assuming an expression of bright interest in everything, she resolutely avoided Jenny's anxious gaze. She laughed a great deal and only she knew it was sometimes close to hysteria.

And she hid her lack of appetite too, pushing the asparagus mousse around her plate, rearranging the fresh lobster, hiding slices of tournedos of beef beneath the wild mushrooms from the Veneto and managing successfully to taste very little of the sorbet.

The cheese and parfait she left alone but accepted a Turkish coffee and iced water, realising that her head was spinning. In an attempt to blank out Rozzano's betrayal, she'd taken too much of the different wines which had accompanied each course. A little too late, she realised she needed to keep her wits about her if she was to stay one jump ahead of the deceitful Rozzano.

After the guests had opened their gifts of crystal clocks and gold pens—or carefully chosen toys in the case of the children—the speeches began. Sophia listened to the praise heaped on her fickle husband's head and her anger intensified.

He'd deceived all these good people. Minor European princes and princesses, counts and lords, maids, boatmen

157

and shrewd businessmen. All had fallen for his charismatic charm. What chance had there been for her to evade his silver tongue?

Wondering if her brilliant smile would freeze on her face, she began to plot her revenge in earnest, hating herself for what she was doing—but hating him far, far more.

They flew in Rozzano's executive jet from the small private airport on the Lido, arriving at their honeymoon destination a short while later. Rozzano had offered her the choice to go anywhere in the world. She had asked to stay in his sixteenth-century summer palace: a Palladian villa in the Veneto, the mainland to the north of Venice—'terra firma', as Rozzano called it.

The villa had sounded very romantic. On the fourth of June, for about four hundred years, the Barsinis had packed all their furniture, tapestries and possessions and barged them up to Villa Barsini to escape the threat of malaria from the canals—though there was no such danger nowadays. Here, he'd assured her, a small, discreet staff would ensure their total privacy.

For a brief moment at the reception, she'd hovered on the brink of demanding that Rozzano should go alone and leave her at Ca' D'Antiga. But she'd immediately imagined her grandfather's surprise and the questions he'd ask. She couldn't do that to him. He adored Rozzano and she didn't want to be the one who enlightened him as to his grandson-in-law's true nature.

Her grandfather must never know that there was anything wrong with her marriage. Her heart sank. That meant that for the rest of her grandfather's life she'd have to act a lie. It was too appalling to contemplate.

The present was bad enough. As they drove between

the huge cast-iron gates towards the villa, the thought of being alone with Rozzano day after day filled her with horror. Without love, without the deep friendship she'd believed they'd shared, the long days and nights would drag.

Agitated, she fidgeted with the skirt of her Valentino suit, suddenly hating its Barsini green and gold. Her eyes blazed. They were colours she'd never wear again!

'Won't be long, darling,' Rozzano said, in cheerful ignorance of her mood.

She stretched her mouth into a smile and nodded, pretending an interest in the surrounding parkland. What ever would she do with herself for a week? Gloomily she supposed that she could get up late, spend her days walking and swimming and go to bed early.

The one consolation was that it wouldn't be for long. They had both been eager to begin their married life in the D'Antiga palace. Her stomach lurched with intense misery. She'd had such dreams of their rosy future. And now her marriage was nothing but a sham.

The scenery became a blur as her thoughts tumbled in confusion. Desperately she battled for composure as Rozzano enthusiastically pointed out the deer, the place where he used to hide when his father had beaten him, the beautiful view across the valley...

'You were beaten?' she said, suddenly picking up on what he'd said.

He grimaced. 'I tended to be too exuberant for Father's liking, too ready to show how I felt.'

A beaten child often became violent to others... 'And what did your mother think about this?' she asked, cold to the bone.

'I don't know. She supported my father,' he replied, as if that were the most natural thing in the world.

'Did she love you?' Sophia asked, wondering nervously what Rozzano would do when she refused to provide him with an heir. She looked at the strength of his arms and shoulders and shrank back into the seat.

'I've no idea,' he mused. 'I hardly knew her.'

This was the first time he'd spoken of his mother. Up to now, he'd always changed the subject. Curious to understand the relationship between mother and son, Sophia asked quietly, 'She cuddled you?'

'Never. I had plenty of affection from my English nanny and English governess, though. Most aristos employ English tutors for their children—that's why we all speak English so well. Don't worry,' he said, stroking her hand where it picked anxiously at her jacket hem. 'We won't be remote from our children.'

'No,' she agreed bleakly. 'We won't.' And omitted to add that there wouldn't be any. She swallowed, fearing the moment she'd have to tell him.

'Look, this is my favourite view of the lake,' he said eagerly. 'I'll take you to the island on it. We'll have a picnic if the weather stays warm enough.'

She must have made some kind of response that satisfied him because he continued driving. But she was thinking about his upbringing and how it had made him the man he was, outwardly suave and smooth, inwardly repressed and angry, with a flagrant disregard for the notion that love and marriage went hand in hand.

She should have listened to Letizia. Rozzano's attitude was indeed bred in the bone. She trembled. The deed was done. She was irrevocably married and she would have to prepare herself for a different sort of marriage from the one she'd expected. Perhaps, she thought soberly, it would be better never to daydream again, then she would never be disappointed by reality.

Pale and wan, she stepped from the limousine, her tension softening a little as she gazed at the beautiful building. It had a classically Roman appearance with graceful columns, domes and a portico.

In that moment, Sophia understood how completely Rozzano had been steeped in history. Every step he took had been trodden by his ancestors.

It was hardly surprising that preserving the past had become more important to him than living for the present. In his mind, the survival of the family had to take precedence over its individuals, whatever the cost. He'd been forced to sacrifice his jealously guarded freedom to marry her. She'd put her trust and her heart in the care of a man who didn't deserve either.

Her stomach swooped. He'd be furious that his sacrifice had been in vain. A shiver ran the length of her body.

At the moment, he was all smiles and being hugged by the staff as if he were a long-lost son. She found a smile and pasted it to her face.

'Buon giorno. Che piacere incontraria,' she said, beginning her greetings in hesitant Italian. And she too was enveloped in loving arms and found herself being passed from one delighted person to another. And, desperate for love and affection, she responded warmly, while everyone exclaimed extravagantly over her clothes, her hair, and her beauty.

'So lovely! Ah, *principe*, she has the face of a Madonna!' declared a man who must surely be the gardener.

'I know,' he said softly, disengaging himself from an extraordinarily emotional embrace with a tall and stately woman with steel-grey hair. He put his arm around Sophia and caressed her cheek. 'I don't deserve her at all.'

When he translated that, he was met by a chorus of protests.

'The husband, he is a good man,' confided a jolly woman in a starched apron. 'Maddy! *In inglese.*'

The grey-haired woman smiled happily. 'I'm Maddy Clark; I used to be Rozzano's nanny. Welcome, *principessa*, and congratulations. I'm sure you'll be very happy together.'

Sophia accepted Maddy's hug and kisses in amazement. 'Thank you. I'm glad to meet you. Rozzano's talked about you so much.'

The look Maddy gave to Rozzano spoke volumes. She adored him; that was clear. 'I knew it would take a special woman to capture Rozzano's love,' she said quietly. 'From what he's said about *you*,' she added, her eyes twinkling, 'I know he's found her. And I can only tell you that you'll never find a kinder, more thoughtful, more loving man—'

'Maddy! Please!' Rozzano implored, looking embarrassed. 'You two can compare notes another time.'

He began to speak to his staff in Italian. Maddy saw Sophia's lack of comprehension and translated for Sophia's benefit.

'He's thanking everyone for getting the villa ready,' Maddy said. 'He knows it's taken a lot of work. And he's promising that you'll wear your wedding dress for them to see—and that we'll all have a small reception here in compensation.' She sighed. 'He's so thoughtful. Always was. What a wonderful life you will have together!'

Sophia's eyes misted over. Fortunately Maddy thought she was being sentimental, because she smiled and patted her shoulder understandingly.

'Claim your bride,' she said to Rozzano.

Smiling happily, he swept Sophia off her feet and carried her over the threshold to the sound of applause. Everyone loved him, she thought bleakly. Did he never show his dark side to anyone but her?

Her pulses raced as he continued on, up a grand staircase. 'Maddy should have come to the wedding,' she said, blurting out the first thing she could think of.

'She's terrified of crowds,' he explained. 'She's stayed here ever since I grew too old for her care. Are you all right, darling? You seem to be shivering.'

Looking concerned, he hurried on and set her down in the bridal suite, his hands resting lightly on her shoulders. And she remembered how a long, long time ago she'd wondered what this moment would be like in a marriage of convenience. Now she knew.

A fit of nerves started her teeth chattering. 'I'm cold,' she said feebly.

His eyes kindled. 'I'll warm you.'

'No!' She backed away, her eyes wide with terror.

'Sophia, sweetheart!' he coaxed, taking a step towards her.

'Don't come any nearer!' she cried in panic.

He raised his hands and stayed put. 'Why don't you have a bath?' he suggested gently. 'I'll shower and we can—'

'Yes. A bath.'

'Poor darling!' he crooned understandingly. 'It's been quite a day! You were wonderful, Sophia. When I turned and saw you for the first time, you looked so beautiful that I thought my heart—'

'I'll have that bath,' she mumbled abruptly, her voice high and unnatural.

'Sure.' He reached out and drew her quaking body to his. The kiss was sweet and tormenting, gentle enough not to be a threat, but igniting her nevertheless. 'That's better,' he murmured into her hair. 'See you in a short time, mmm? The bathroom's in there. All your things are ready for you.'

She fled and shut the door behind her in relief. Her legs wouldn't hold her and she slumped to the floor. It was his warm and loving voice she couldn't bear. The adoration in his eyes. The tender smile on his devastatingly handsome, treacherous, *vile* face.

Limply she struggled to her feet and searched for a key or a bolt to lock the door. There was nothing. But then it was a bridal suite and brides weren't supposed to keep their husbands out.

Resigned, she tore off the hated suit and flung it into a corner. Tears streamed down her face as she kicked off the pretty, glove-soft stilettos, which she'd so admired. They'd go in the bin tomorrow, she vowed grimly.

Almost blinded by tears, she reached out to turn on the taps. While the water ran into the deep marble bath, she scrubbed at her eyes with the back of her hand and stared down at herself miserably. She'd chosen her underwear with loving care, thinking of the moment when Rozzano would run his hands over the sensuous satin briefs and bra. She'd imagined him kneeling at her feet, slowly unfastening her suspenders and sliding the sexy lace-topped stockings down, kissing every inch of exposed skin as he did so.

Instead, he'd had more than his fill of lace-topped stockings for one day and here she was, undressing herself.

As she would for... She winced. How many years of emptiness would there be? The cold, loveless days stretched ahead with a terrifying certainty. She didn't know if she'd have the strength of mind to sustain her decision to remain in a loveless marriage.

She dragged her teeth over her lip to silence the terrible pain inside her. She had to stop wishing for that golden future she'd expected as her right, and face facts. Between now and the end of her bath, she had to accept what had happened and plan her own future.

CHAPTER NINE

TURNING off the taps, she found her favourite bath oil on an elegant Georgian table and added it to the water, doing her best to ignore her delicate lace nightdress and peignoir on the nearby chaise longue. They'd been chosen with such care. Such joy.

She stepped into the bath and looked around, scowling. Oil paintings hung on the walls, silver candelabra romantically lit the room, a central chandelier in Venetian glass sent rainbow colours from its sparkling crystal facets. Even the darn bathroom was filled with relics of the past! she thought bitterly. And she'd become just another part of Barsini tradition. A baby machine.

'Not this time!' she muttered rebelliously at the watching ancestors.

She lay in the bath, miserable and angry at the same time. Every now and then she'd feel cold and she'd top up the water, adding a little more of the subtly perfumed oils she'd come to adore. She could have luxury for the rest of her life. But it was worth nothing without Rozzano's love.

The love she craved must come from elsewhere. From children. She would revert to her old life of caring for the underprivileged—but this time she'd have the money to fund her plans.

'Sophia?'

'Not ready!' she croaked.

'I am.'

The door opened. Hastily she slid under the silky blue

water as he entered. Her eyes rounded. He was wearing a towel and nothing else. The hunger rose in her body, shortening her breath. And a savage pain seared through her quaking frame.

She had to tell him. Before it was too late.

'I wondered if you were all right,' he said fondly.

'Shattered.' Horrified at the frightened little whisper, she closed her eyes and hoped he'd take the hint. 'Headache.'

'It's not surprising. I'll give you a massage. Come on,' he murmured, his voice unnervingly close. 'I'll help you out and get you into bed—'

'No, Rozzano, I—'

She gasped, her eyes snapping open at the touch of his hand on her breast. A groan escaped her before she could stop it and he kissed her open mouth luxuriantly while his hand slid over the swell of her soapy breast, making her moan and writhe in need.

'Are you teasing me? I do believe you are!' he said softly into her mouth. 'Witch! I'll make you regret that!'

His fingers were everywhere, tormenting her, making her cling to him helplessly. And then she was being lifted into the air and carried, still dripping, into the bedroom.

Every time she fought to speak, he silenced her with bruising, passionate kisses. She quaked as he slid her onto the sandwashed silk sheets. He was intensely aroused and so was she, however unwillingly. And she loathed herself for betraying herself so easily.

Frantically her body slid beneath his in an attempt to wriggle free. Laughing, he pinned her with his weight and with a groan of anguish she grabbed his face and ground her mouth against his, hating, wanting, despising, needing him with a passion that terrified her.

The smooth glide of his hands over her wet, fevered

body was sending her mad with frustration. Her glittering eyes met his and she bucked in shock that he could still maintain that glib pretence of loving desire. Furious with his duplicity, she felt compelled to move her body fiercely beneath him for some kind of physical relief because she knew that she would be forever a virgin, forever childless. And that terrible injustice hurt her beyond belief.

Distraught, she gave an involuntary wail of despair, which caused him to freeze.

'Sophia, darling, what is it?' he asked hoarsely.

Sobbing, she fought him, beating her fists against his chest and feeling empty and ashamed that she should still love him despite everything she knew.

'I hate you!' she screamed hysterically, wrenching this way and that as he caught her wrists and pushed her arms over her head. Frightened and vulnerable, her nude body horrifyingly available to him, she stared in terror at his shocked face and realised that revenge wasn't sweet at all. It was agony.

'Please don't hurt me!' she begged. 'Just leave me alone!'

When he flinched but made no other response, she let out a shuddering sob and said in a cold, dead voice, 'Let me go, Rozzano. It's all over between us.'

He tried to speak but seemed too dazed. Amazingly, she felt sorry for him—actually wanted to comfort him! She was mad. Had he thought of her when he'd gone off to find Arabella on the day of his wedding? Had he given a damn about his bride when he'd eased off Arabella's lacy-topped stockings—which, she reminded herself in rage, were just like the ones *she* wore because *he* adored them?

'Traitor! Get off me!' she seethed, beside herself with

misery. 'Get off before I scream the place down and ruin your damn reputation!'

Like an automaton he obeyed. Reached for his robe and knotted the belt. Stood staring at her as if he were in some slow-moving nightmare.

'I don't understand,' he said dully.

'Don't you?' she scathed, scrabbling to sit up and pulling the sheet over her.

It was embroidered with violets, she thought bleakly. They could have been making love here in this lovely four-poster, easing the ache in their bodies, confirming their commitment to one another. They would have slept afterwards, and then in the morning they would have snuggled into each other's arms and discussed their plans for the day and for the rest of their lives...

Damn herself for putting herself through such self-torture! She wouldn't daydream again! The cold, hard reality of the future was hers—and hers alone.

'Sophia!' Evidently confused, he ran a hand through his dishevelled hair, his face tight with strain. *'Explain!'* he jerked out passionately. 'What do you think you're doing?'

'It's simple,' she said in a low tone. She drew in a long breath from her cramped lungs. 'Think, Rozzano. What is your worst nightmare?'

'That you should cease to love me,' he rasped without hesitation.

She almost faltered. He was so slick, so quick with the right answer that she would have been convinced if it hadn't been for the evidence of her own eyes.

'No,' she said bitterly. 'That's not it. Try *childlessness.* I'm your means to an heir. *That's* your dream, isn't it?'

There was a coldness about his face now, the aristocratic features taking on a hard, chiselled appearance.

'You know I want us to have children,' he replied, without emotion.

Her mouth curled in contempt. Now they were getting to the real man, to the coat-of-arms heart that sat inside his damn princely body, crushing any stray feelings that might ruin his wretched game plan!

'You want them so badly that you'd sell your soul to the devil to get them!' she ground out.

His dark eyes flared with anger and then were veiled. 'I don't know what you mean,' he said stiffly.

'Yes, you do!' Impatient with the throbbing of her head, she sat up and grimly pulled out all the pins holding her hair. As it tumbled down to her shoulders in angry, bouncing waves, she flashed a malevolent glance at him and said, 'Get this straight, Rozzano. I won't ever have your children. Not unless you intend to rape me!'

He felt a roaring in his ears as her words struck him like a death-blow. And the past came back to destroy him. He couldn't speak, couldn't move. It couldn't happen, he told himself, fighting for sanity. Not again.

His brain refused to function. There was only the raw nightmare, filling his head with an unbearable insistence. To escape it, he had to move, do something. Fight his way back to normality.

'Rozzano!'

Her shocked scream brought him out of his daze. He looked down at his bleeding hand, clenched in a fist, and the shattered crystal goblets on the table. With a muttered curse at his blind stupidity, he strode to one of the basins in the room and stuck his fist under the cold tap.

She was by his side. Naked and damp beneath the hastily donned bathrobe. Smelling delicious. Warm, infinitely desirable. He jammed his teeth together, refusing to give way to his instincts which demanded that he

should turn to her, take her in his arms and kiss the nightmare away.

'Is there any glass in your cuts?' she asked anxiously.

'I don't know.' And he didn't much care.

'Let me look—'

'No, Sophia!' He saw her flinch at his roar and began
to examine his hand, knowing he must control himself
whatever the provocation.

'I have some tweezers, if—'

'Not necessary.' He took the scrubbing brush and some
soap and swept the wounds, glad of the pain.

Sophia had cried out as if his action had hurt her too.
Her hand had gone to her mouth and she'd looked
shocked by his extreme action. He wrapped a linen cloth
tightly around his fist and blessed the diversion. Now he
could show composure, regardless of the fear he felt in
his heart.

'Right,' he said grimly, turning to face her. 'What lies
has Enrico been spinning now?'

She took several steps back, her expression cold and
hurt. 'None.'

'Then—'

'I saw you!' she spat. 'Stripping Arabella at *my* wedding reception!'

He started. 'How—?'

'What the hell does it matter *how*?' she yelled. 'You
were making love to her a few hours after your *marriage*!
You *rat*! Couldn't you have been more discreet? Couldn't
you have *pretended* we were happily married—?'

'I didn't make love to her!' he snapped, appalled by
what she was saying. 'I was telling her to get dressed—'

'Liar!'

'It's true, dammit!'

'It didn't look like that to me! And you can deny it

till you're blue in the face but I won't believe you! I should never have married you! But you wove your web of lies and charmed me as you charm everyone. You've got your bride. You don't need to worry that she's a gold-digger. Unfortunately, your bride has cottoned on to the kind of man you are and she doesn't love you *at all*.'

'You desire me,' he drawled, ruthlessly killing his stunned reaction stone-dead.

'If you think I'm going to sleep with you for sex alone, then you don't know me!' she blazed.

'Why not? You want children!' he shot out, before he could stop himself.

She flinched. 'You *brute*!' she cried hoarsely, close to tears.

He was furious with himself for speaking without thinking. But he realised that he'd been harbouring the hope that if he could get her into bed they could heal their differences.

'We have common desires,' he said, more controlled now.

'Yes. I'd love to have babies!' she cried. 'You're the one who's taken that choice away from me! Now I'll have to be content with caring for other people's children, working in an orphanage, setting one up perhaps. It'll be some consolation, Rozzano—but it won't be what I want!'

'Then come to bed with me.' He let his hunger for her burn in his eyes. She shuddered, her mouth sweetly sensual as her tongue slicked over her parted lips. Desperate to grab her, he took a steadying breath and began to fight for his dream. 'We're both tired. For the sake of appearances we must sleep in this room. Lie in my arms and let's talk this out.'

'No!' She wrapped her robe tightly around her as if to

shut him out for ever. 'I've decided what I want our future to be, Rozzano.'

'Have you, indeed?'

'In public, we'll be like any normal, happily married couple. For my grandfather's sake only. Not for your family honour or your darn pride!'

'And in private?' he enquired, a terrible coldness stealing through every vein in his body.

'You don't touch me. No sex. No sly caresses. Nothing! And you'll take no part in D'Antiga business from now on. You have your own business to run. I intend to get involved in charity work, especially in orphanages. That's where my future lies, Rozzano. As for yours, you can do what you darn well please, providing you don't hurt Grandfather. Now, perhaps you'd like to take a pillow and make yourself comfortable on the sofa.'

He stared at her aghast. She'd worked everything out. Her eyes blazed with a hatred that sliced deep into his cold body and he could see that she was adamant. But he had to make one final effort.

'I married you,' he said hoarsely, 'with one thing in mind—'

'Yes!' she spat. 'The future of the house of Barsini! Wealth marries wealth. Very convenient. Well, I've had it up to *here* with your family!' she cried, slashing her hand across her throat in a violent gesture. 'The past is *history*—'

'I can't avoid it,' he said tightly. 'I live in it, day by day.'

'I know,' she muttered. 'And you're all so wrapped up in your noble past that you forget to live in the present—'

'No, Sophia.' He'd taken three strides and was in front of her before he knew what he was doing. Tormented by her beauty, he hardened his eyes so that he didn't betray himself. 'I honour the past, but I live for now. I wouldn't be a successful businessman otherwise,' he said harshly. 'This matter between us is to do with trust. And you don't choose to trust me, do you?'

'No. Because,' she said tremulously, her eyes shining with unshed tears, 'I've realised that you put your dynasty above everything else.'

'That's not true!' he denied vehemently. 'Whoever told you—'

'Oh, stop it, Rozzano!' she yelled, clapping her hands to her ears. 'I won't listen to your slick lies any more!'

He could see that she had reached the end of her tether. Tomorrow she would be calmer. His eyes glittered. And he'd find out what devils had got into his bride.

Without a word, he picked up one of the pillows from the bed and flung it on the sofa. Grimly he gathered up the cream linen coverlet and settled himself down for the night. Correction. Until Sophia fell asleep. He had no intention of spending his wedding night any other way than that which he'd planned: making love to his wife.

Curled up in a self-pitying ball, Sophia waited for sleep. But, tired though she was, she couldn't relax. Her mind kept re-enacting in excruciating detail all the events of the day, which had been initially euphoric, finally a living hell.

It was a long time later when she heard him move. Holding her breath, she listened. His footfalls were approaching. Life leapt into her listless body, demanding that she should satisfy its urges, and she despaired that she would ever get over her physical infatuation for him. The bed depressed behind her.

'Don't *touch* me!' she warned furiously, screwing herself up even tighter.

'This is my bed,' he growled. 'I'm damn well sleeping in it!'

Hastily she moved to the edge and lay there, hanging on to the mattress, her stiff body defying him to come anywhere near her.

She fell asleep in the early hours of the morning. He'd been tuned in to her breathing and recognised the deeper, slower inhalations as she gradually relaxed. Very carefully, he rolled over.

In the moonlight he could see the outline of her figure. The curve of her waist, the swell of her hip. His heart pounded heavily. Perhaps sensing the crackling tension of his body, she stirred and turned to face him, her eyes seemingly soft with love. Amazingly, she smiled and touched his mouth with an enquiring finger.

Hardly daring to breathe, he tentatively peeled back the sheet, expecting her to stop him at any moment. She didn't. Taut with longing, he let his eyes feed on the graceful curves of her body, and marvelled at its beauty. Still she made no move to discourage him. Hope surged through him. She loved him. Everything would be all right.

Every bone and muscle in his body strained under the ruthlessness of his restraint. He wanted to fling himself on her, kiss her passionately, make her truly his wife... Instead, he softly feathered his fingers over her warm, satiny shoulders, at her gentle sigh, he put his face close to her neck and breathed in her fragrance.

Sophia accepted his hesitant kisses along the curve of her jaw, giving out little gasps of pleasure which made him groan with relief. His cautious hand moved to the curve of her breast. The nipple was already hard beneath his fingers. A shock of desire rocketed through him and he could hold back no longer, clasping her fiercely in his arms, his mouth descending passionately on hers.

Sophia responded immediately, matching his passion as they tumbled over the bed, hungrily grasping one another and straining to press even closer. She twisted and turned against him, using her body to take the edge off her terrible need.

Then, and almost too late, she realised that she must never obey the desires of her heart or her body. Her head had to rule. Nothing else. He was worthless.

'No! Stop!' she cried vehemently, managing to wriggle away. His eyes were brilliant and fierce, blazing with desire. She stared at him, forcing herself to deny him. 'Leave me alone!' she said in a horrified whisper.

'But... You can't do this to me!' he hissed savagely. 'You can't encourage me and— I don't understand! I never thought you'd play the tease—'

Appalled, she hugged her throbbing body, her eyes dark with pain. A few moments later and he would have consummated the marriage. 'You can't sleep in the same bed as me!' she ranted, half in anger, half anguished by her hopeless love for him. 'I won't have you sneaking up and raping me in the middle of the night! I won't—!'

'*Basta*! If you think that of me—!'

His face twisted in torment, he swung his legs to the floor and dragged on his robe. In fear, she watched him striding up and down, seeing the scorching anger in every rigid step he took. His mouth had become hard and grim and she could see from the way his chest heaved that he was dangerously close to losing control.

'So!' he spat, his eyes black with hatred. 'I've done it again!'

Cowering beneath the sheet, she blinked in confusion. 'What?'

He stopped, contempt pouring from his whole body. 'You don't know. No one does. I don't make it a habit to tell the world about my secrets. Especially my humiliation—'

'You brought this on yourself!' she shot at him.

'By marrying again?' He gave a harsh, humourless laugh. 'Perhaps. But I didn't expect my *second* wife to ban me from her bed. At least,' he growled, 'Nicoletta allowed me to make love to her on our wedding night and for a while after!'

Sophia stared. Her heart thudded loudly. 'Did she disapprove of your infidelity? What did you expect?' she scathed.

Rozzano frowned as if puzzled. '*My* infidelity? Far from it. Hers! She banned me because she didn't want children to spoil her figure,' he said contemptuously. 'Unknown to me, she aborted her first child and wouldn't let me touch her after that.'

He was lying, though she couldn't fathom why. Pity, perhaps? 'I think you've forgotten something. She did become pregnant again—that's why she died. You must have been together as man and wife...'

Her voice trailed away. He looked ashen, his eyes tiny pinpoints of pain.

'No. She had an affair with Enrico,' he said hoarsely.

Sophia clutched at her breast in horror.

'The child was his. A *mistake*, he told me. She tried to abort it in secret in some clinic in South America. Developed septicaemia. And died.'

The silence was crushing. He'd kept this secret locked up inside of him, pretending that everything was fine between Enrico and himself for the sake of...his wretched family. Sophia drew in a long, despairing breath. How could she say what she felt? That her heart went out to him, that she couldn't imagine how he'd lived day by day, knowing his brother had indirectly killed his beloved wife?

'I don't know what to say,' she whispered. 'To love someone and be betrayed—'

'I didn't love her by then,' he broke in curtly. 'I'd discovered how shallow and grasping she was. Well, Sophia. It seems...' he grunted, bitter humour twisting his mouth. '...history repeats itself. This time, however, I refuse to let a woman destroy my life. Do what you damn well please. I won't attempt to make love to you again.'

At least, thought Sophia towards the end of the week, he'd been true to his word. With an almost inhuman control of his features, he'd outlined the rules. One: as she'd suggested, they were to be affectionate in public. Two: during their honeymoon he'd pretend to be teaching her to ride. When they were out of sight of the house, he would leave her to her own devices. He would return after his ride and they would arrive back at the house together. Three: he would sleep on the sofa. Four: when they were back in Venice, they would discuss the future in detail.

With little sleep, little food that week and tension gripping every muscle in her body, Sophia felt dog-weary. It was their last day at the villa and she'd been power-walking for over two hours, punishing her body in an attempt to blank out her mind.

Hearing the thunder of hooves, she rose from the tree stump where she'd been waiting, intending to mount her tethered palomino. Before she could do so, a sudden attack of giddiness assailed Sophia and she swayed, clutching at a tree for support.

'Are you ill?' came Rozzano's urgent voice, from far, far away.

Darkness was spiralling all around her. She felt his arms holding her up and gradually the fog cleared. 'No,' she whispered. 'I think I got up too quickly.'

She swallowed, shaken by his nearness. As usual when riding, he wore just breeches and boots and an open-necked white shirt. His body was slicked with sweat and tiny trickles of moisture were dripping from his tousled wet hair. He'd been punishing himself too, she mused vaguely.

'You haven't been eating much. You need a good meal inside you,' he growled.

Weakly she leaned her head back against the trunk of the tree. 'That's it. I didn't have any dinner last night, or breakfast this morning. I'll be all right once I've...'

Her voice had become a hoarse croak. His warm breath had sensitised her lips, making them open in an instinctive invitation.

They stood there for an eternity, it seemed, his body against hers, pressing her to the tree, his strength and warmth infinitely desirable. She felt too weak to fight the demands of her heart and went limp in his grasp.

For a brief second his mouth drove brutally into hers, bringing her back to pulsating life again. Then he had stepped back and was wiping his mouth with the back of his hand as if it were contaminated.

'I'll ride back on my own today,' he rasped, his face consumed with anger. 'I'll send a groom out for you—'

'No.' Miserably she stumbled towards her pony. 'I'll come.'

She attempted to mount and didn't seem to have the

strength. With a muttered imprecation, Rozzano strode forward and cupped his hands. Close to tears, she placed her small booted foot there, and he tipped her easily into the saddle.

They returned in silence. One day, she thought, I will surrender in a weak moment. And I'll hate myself for evermore.

As was their custom, they stood with their arms around one another chatting to the groom. The tension in her neck and shoulders screamed for Rozzano's magic touch to ease her muscles. The ache in her body begged for something more fundamental and primitive.

Somehow she kept up an inane chatter during the lunch he forced her to eat, and then at last she was free to wander in the garden alone. In the privacy of the summer house she opened one of the lace-curtained windows for air and curled up on the cushions of a huge cane chair beside it, trying to concentrate on her plans for the orphanage.

Until she heard Arabella, calling Rozzano's name.

He whirled around, his hackles up. He'd wanted to find Sophia, to know how she was, and here was Arabella—the cause of his problems! He leant against the summerhouse veranda and eyed her narrowly.

'What the hell are you doing here?' he demanded in a hard tone.

She looked scared, but came towards him nevertheless. 'I came to apologise.'

'For what?' he scathed. 'Seducing my brother on my wedding day? Or for being one of his mistresses for the past two years?'

'I've been his *only* mistress for six months,' she defended. 'I know what you think of me,' she went on more quietly. 'I did try to do what you said—to prevent scandal by pretending an interest in anyone other than Enrico. Letizia was fooled—she thought I had designs on you—'

'She's your friend,' he said coldly. 'How could you deceive her?'

'I can't help who I love, Rozzano!' she declared passionately. 'Can you?'

He clenched his teeth to deaden the pain. 'No.'

'I didn't set out to hurt anyone. But I am deeply sorry for what we did at your wedding. We were both rather drunk, but it was still unforgivable.' She hung her head. 'I felt ashamed when you stood there, handing me my clothes as if you didn't even trust me to get dressed without supervision.'

'If I hadn't come in and stopped you both,' he said in contempt, 'you would have committed adultery in Alberto's house. How could you? You were guests at my wedding—'

'Yes, but we're crazy about one another! Don't you know what it's like not to touch the person you love?'

He couldn't answer for several seconds. Even then, when he spoke his voice betrayed how he felt. 'Yes. I know.'

'Forgive us. But we do love each other.' She hesitated. 'I've come to say goodbye. Enrico and I are going away together.'

He let out a hiss of surprise. 'And Letizia?'

'She cares only for money. Enrico will give her a good settlement. And perhaps she'll find someone she loves too. It's better than living a lie, Rozzano! You have to admit that!'

But he wouldn't meet her eyes because she was right. 'You know he can't be faithful,' he cautioned, beginning to think that perhaps Arabella was the right woman for Enrico with her guts and determination.

'I do know. I'm willing to take that chance. He's not strong, like you. But few men can be, Rozzano. You're too big an icon for him to live up to. Maybe in England he'll stop trying to prove he can do just one thing better than you, and learn to be himself. I'll make something of us both. One day you'll be proud of your brother. I promise you that. I'm only sorry that you haven't found someone to love—'

He winced. 'Don't believe everything you hear.' Suddenly he wanted to rid himself of all the lies, the pretences he'd nursed for the whole of his life. 'Arabella, I know that on my wedding day I told you and Enrico what my feelings were for Sophia. But I lied to protect her. I…love Sophia more than my own life. I thought that if Rico knew that he'd hurt her to get his own back on me. So I said I'd married her because she was suitable and I wanted an heir. Whereas…' his voice deepened '…she's the most important person to me on this earth. I value her above everything.'

'I don't understand your motives for lying, but I'm glad. Perhaps both the Barsini brothers will be happy at last,' Arabella said quietly. She kissed him on the cheek. 'Goodbye. God bless you. Be happy.'

He didn't move for a long time. His heart felt like stone, his limbs leaden. 'Be happy'. As if.

He covered his face, his hands shaking uncontrollably. Thank God no one could see him. He drew in a raw, painful breath and wiped a small tear from his eye. He'd abandon his intended search for Sophia. What was the point? He couldn't put himself through that torture again. Every second in her company was agony. He couldn't wait for the time when they began to lead separate lives.

*　　*　　*

Devastated, Sophia watched him through the heavy lace curtains. He'd lied to Enrico because he'd feared that the past would be repeated, and his brother would try to seduce her.

She had wronged Rozzano terribly. Almost ruined them both. Paralysed with shock, she felt a huge lump of emotion fill her throat. It was so hard and painful that she couldn't call out and stop him from walking away as if the world sat on his shoulders.

He loved her. Arabella had never been interested in him—or he in Arabella. Everything he'd said had been true and she'd chosen not to believe him. His staff and friends had greater faith than she did. Appalled, she followed his slow progress along the lakeside. He stumbled and her heart leapt with compassion.

Perhaps he would forgive her. Suddenly life came back to her shocked body and she jumped to her feet, flying out of the summer house towards him.

'Rozzano!' she yelled, half sobbing as she ran. 'Stop, Rozzano!'

He spun around in alarm. 'What's happened? Who's hurt you?'

'*I've* hurt me!' she wailed, coming to a halt a few feet away, the tears streaming down her face.

'Where?' he demanded, frowning.

'Here,' she sobbed, her hand on her heart. 'And I've hurt you—'

'I thought you'd been injured,' he muttered. 'Cut the dramatics. I'm not in the mood. Leave me in peace!'

Panting and distraught, she struggled to master her tears and speak coherently. 'But Rozz—' she began jerkily.

'Leave me! For God's sake, see when you're not wanted!' he snarled, striding rapidly away.

'You do want me!' she cried, running to his side and grabbing his arm.

He shook her off. But said nothing, forging on, his face thunderous.

'I want you,' she whispered.

His stride checked, then continued. But she'd shaken him.

Her hand stole to his chest. He brushed it away. She slid it around his strong back and he flinched.

'What are you trying to do?' he snarled, coming to an abrupt halt.

He sounded like a wounded animal. She stared into his blazing, pain-filled eyes and let out a shuddering breath. There was one way to prove her trust in him. Slowly she began to unbutton her shirt.

She had his attention. His gaze searched hers warily as if she might be deliberately tormenting him. He made no move to touch her but stood tensely, an arm's length away.

Sophia didn't take her eyes from his. Slipping the shirt from her shoulders, she saw the tremor in his jaw and knew he was finding it difficult to remain indifferent. The shirt drifted to the ground. Her fingers reached back for the clasp of her lacy bra and Rozzano gave a satisfyingly sharp intake of breath when that, too, was discarded.

Too intent on gaining his love and forgiveness to even think about her natural inhibitions, she teased him by taking her time over unbuckling the belt of her jodhpurs.

'I need help with the boots,' she breathed, nerves and sexual hunger making her voice husky. This had to work. He mustn't turn away in cold pride and ruin their future. Shaking with sheer desperation, she braced her naked back against the smooth trunk of a eucalyptus tree and lifted one booted leg invitingly.

As if in a dream, he swallowed hard then knelt to ease first one, then the other boot from her feet. But he stood up again, still keeping his distance as if he didn't totally trust her.

Sophia felt panic rise within her. She would have to lure him still further. Wriggling the jodhpurs down, she tossed them away and stood naked but for a pair of tiny red lace briefs. Her breasts felt tight and hard, every inch of her skin tingled with sensation. Her body was ready for him and he must know it.

'Make love to me,' she murmured.

He didn't move an inch. But there had been a small, betraying twitch of his jaw and a flicker of his lowered lashes. Sophia lifted her arms above her head and pulled her hair from its confining snood. Gulping at her own audacity, she let her fingers drift down over her breasts.

'I want to have your child,' she told him huskily, her heart melting at the struggle going on within him. 'I love you, Rozzano. I know you weren't unfaithful to me. I want to apologise for doubting you. I misunderstood what I saw. I heard Arabella talking to you outside the summer house. Oh, please, please forgive me!' she begged.

She was in his arms in a moment, being crushed in his impassioned embrace. 'Sophia!' he rasped in her ear. 'Of course I forgive you! I'd have doubted you under the same circumstances. The evidence was damning. My darling! I thought I'd lost you—'

Her tear-stained face lifted to his. 'I love you so much! I couldn't bear to think of life without your love—'

'Nor I without yours,' he said rawly. 'I think I fell in love with you straight away. I didn't realise till later. It wasn't like anything I'd ever felt before. I thought I was acting rationally, scheming and plotting because I needed an heir and you seemed perfect to be my wife. And then, when we were in London and you said we must part, I felt devastated. Even then I couldn't admit the truth: that I loved you. Yet I wanted to protect you, care for you, keep you with me day and night, every second of the day. Whenever we were separated I felt as if something was missing. It was: a part of my heart. I fell madly in love with you, Sophia, despite all my efforts to stop that happening. I still am in love with you. I love you more than anything in the whole of my life.'

She began to undo the buttons of his shirt. 'Show me,' she whispered. *'Now.'*

Tenderly he drew her down to the grassy bank. Her eyes closed as his mouth met hers. She felt the welcome warmth of his strong body and yielded to the instincts of her heart. Rozzano loved her as much as she loved him. Joy surged in her soul as he brought her closer and closer to their true union. This was a man she could love and honour and respect for the rest of her life.

Afterwards, they watched the setting sun turn the lake to fire. And knew that for them it wasn't the end of a day, but the beginning of a wonderful life together. Happily they returned to the villa, clasping one another frequently on the way, gazing into one another's eyes with profound love.

'I have a confession,' she murmured into the satin warmth of his throat.

'Mmm?' He barely paused in kissing her ear.

'I've always dreamed of being happily married—'

'Mmm.' His mouth found hers.

A breathless while later, she was released. 'And,' she persisted, despite his chuckle, 'there were children in this dream—'

'Uh-huh.'

She gasped as his fingers found the hard tip of her

breast. 'And,' she said, battling for her cause, 'there were *four* children.'

His hand stilled. 'Four.' She nodded and he chuckled. 'Better get on with it, then, hadn't we?'

And, with a total disregard for the people they passed—the gardener, Maddy, who was strolling on the softly lit terrace, and the maid in the hall—he ran hand in hand with Sophia, arriving breathless and exhilarated in the bridal suite.

'Come here, Princess Bride,' he said softly.

She gave her Madonna smile and flung herself into his arms. 'My prince!' she said with a giggle. And he punished her for her mockery in the best possible way she could have imagined.

Coming Next Month

HARLEQUIN PRESENTS®

THE BEST HAS JUST GOTTEN BETTER!

#2055 THE BABY GAMBIT Anne Mather
Matteo di Falco was falling in love with Grace Horton. But it
was Grace's friend who was determined to marry him, by
any means necessary. Matteo was used to getting what he
wanted, and this time he wanted Grace—not her friend!

#2056 THE MISTRESS BRIDE Michelle Reid
(Society Weddings)
The high-profile affair between Sheikh Raschid Al Kadah and
Evie Delahaye was in the media spotlight because their
families were determined to keep them apart. Then Evie
discovered why she *must* marry Raschid....

#2057 HAVING HIS BABIES Lindsay Armstrong
(Expecting!)
Clare had independence, a thriving law firm and a wonderful
lover in Lachlan Hewitt. She knew she loved him, but she
didn't know how he really felt. Then she discovered she was
pregnant. What on earth would Lachlan say?

#2058 MARRIAGE UNDER SUSPICION Sara Craven
The anonymous note suggested that Kate's husband, Ryan,
had betrayed her. Kate was determined to keep her man.
But while their marriage was in jeopardy, there was no way
she'd tell Ryan she was expecting his baby!

#2059 AN ENGAGEMENT OF CONVENIENCE Catherine George
Leo Fortinari seemed to be fooled by Harriet's
impersonation of her friend, Rosa. He'd even agreed to a
pretend engagement with Harriet. But Leo knew that the
woman in his bed wasn't Rosa—for the impostor was a
virgin!

#2060 GIBSON'S GIRL Anne McAllister
Chloe's boss, Gibson Walker, was sinfully gorgeous, but
Chloe had to resist him—she was engaged to someone else!
But the more she ignored him, the more he wanted her.
And soon it became a question of who was seducing
whom....